**Nick Storie Mysteries**
Book 3a
*Better Never Than Late*

Retired gangsters and murder. Nick meets Pancho DeGulio

Critic comment;
Quite good. Above average. Interesting selection of characters. While it's no literary masterpiece, it's not hack, either. Well worth buying. – GGL

# Contents

**Better Never Than Late**

# About the author

CD was born in Lakeland, Florida, in 1938. He is educated in genetics and botany. He has traveled over much of the world, particularly when he was in music as a rock rhythm guitarist with some well-known bands in the late sixties and early seventies. He has worked as a high steel worker and as a longshoreman, clerk, orchidist, bar owner, salvage yard manager and landscaper – among other things.

CD began writing fiction in 1984 and has more than 300 books published as of 3/15/16 in SciFi, murder, orchid culture and various other fields.

He now resides in Puerto Armuelles, David, and Gualaca, Chiriqui, Panamá, where he continues research into epiphytic plants and plays music with friends. He loves the culture of the indigenous people and counts a majority of his closer friends among that group. Several have "adopted" him as their father. He funds those he can afford through the universities where they have all excelled. "The Indios are very intelligent people, they are simply too poor (in material things and money. Culturally, they are very wealthy) to pursue higher education."

CD loves Panamá and the people, despite horrendous experiences (Free e-book; *Fading Paradise*). He plans to spend the rest of his life in the paradise that is Panamá

- Estrelita Suarez V. de Jaramillo – 3/15/2016


CD is involved in research of natural cancer cure at this time. It has proven effective in all cases, so far. It is based on a plant that has been in use for thousands of years, is safe, available, and cheap. He has studied botany, and was cured of a serious lymphoma with use of the plant, *Ambrosia peruviana*.

Information about this cure is free on the FaceBook group, Natural medicine research. CD asks only that all who try it please report on its effectiveness on that group.

## Better Never Than Late

### *Prologue*

Det. Lt. Nathaniel "Nick" Storie finished the status report, sighed deeply, reached for his ever-present cup of strong coffee, and leaned back in the comfortable old wooden chair. Spc. Sgt. Marsha Blevins was just leaving the files, caught his eye, grinned, and held out her hand for the report.

"Marsh, I'm damned glad that one's over," Nick said, with a sour grimace. "I don't think I've ever run across such a crop of nasty people! I'll never understand how anyone can blindly hate like that!"

"It was his father's doing. Both of them. Gruber's father taught him to blindly hate all Jews and Solomon's father taught him to blindly hate all Germans. The only difference in them and us is they took it to ridiculous extremes without thinking.

"Gruber *will* end up in the pen or worse, and you know Solomon is probably going to get the chair.

"It's sad."

"Them and us? What do you mean?"

"Honey Chile, I was taught never to trust no honky-whitey. I don't doubt your father told you never to have nothin' to do with no damned nigger. The difference is we stopped for ten seconds to think about it and both came to the conclusion they were all nuts, anyhow, so we make our own choices.

"It happens to be the way the world is."

"Marsh! I'm shocked! The truth is, my folks were hippies – such as they had around South Florida back then – and taught me all of that crap is just that. Crap!

"That whole mess is starting again in Germany. Lots of Neo-nazis."

"We've got 'em here! Hell! Look at this case! It's what it amounts to!"

She rifled the files, dropped the report into its slot, and closed the drawer.

"What amounts to what?" Capt. James "Paddy" James asked as he came from his office, the "Gloom Room."

He was a huge man, standing six four, and weighing a bit over 250 pounds. He was head of homicide and violent crimes. Marsha was his aide and the actual power behind the office and Nick was night shift homicide detective.

"Nazis. Here," Marsha replied.

"Oh. That," Paddy said. "I'm off, Marsh. I wish you a dull and uneventful night, Nick.

"The wife wants to go to some dumb opera thing tonight and is meeting me in Ft. Myers.

"Want a meal at Miritello's, Marsh? She'll feed the kids and eat at home before she drives out. Why the hell should we drive two cars? Women don't make any sense!"

"Kids?" Nick asked. "They're nineteen and twenty one!" Paddy gave him the finger and said they were both home from college begging for more money – and he told them he would spring for tuition and books, but they could work for anything else.

"You is on for dinner, Honeychile!" Marsha shot back quickly. "I'll call Hank. He can grab the leftover crab chalau crud in the fridge!"

She picked up the desk phone and punched the button for her home number, waited a minute, then said, "Hank? Marsh.

"I hate to break it to you like this. I'm leaving you, so you have to get your own supper ... What? ... Paddy. At Miritello's ... You can heat up the gumbo. In the fridge top ... Hang on."

She punched line two and said, "Violent crimes. M. Blevins ... Where? ... Did you call an ambulance? ... Is she dead? You're absolutely sure? ... Stay there. We're on it. A man will be right there. Don't let anybody come near the body."

She punched line one and said, "Case for Nick, Hank. I'll be in in a couple of hours," and hung up the receiver.

"Nick. Forty seven twelve Parker Place out on Paradise Pointe. Elderly female seems to have fallen down the stairs. Maid says it, quote, `Looks funny, because she was downstairs not more than ten minutes ago and wouldn't have gone up there anyway until after cocktails,' which are what they and the guests are having at the moment.

"The guests don't know anything about it. EMS is on the way.

"Want the lab?"

"I suppose we'd better. Big money out there. Can't miss anything or we'll never hear the end of it."

Marsha punched forensics and said for them to meet Nick at the address as Lt. Jim Hill, day shift homicide, came in to raise an eyebrow at Nick taking the note Marsha was handing him as Nick slipped on his jacket.

January nights could be cold, even in South Florida.

"A 'maybe' at the Pointe – with an `E'," Nick said. "Want to come along?"

"Meet you at Miritello's?" Paddy asked Marsha.

"Woman down the stairs at a party," Marsha said to Jim and, "On my way!" to Paddy.

"I've got a wife to get home to," Jim said. "You should know! Your own wife – as of next month – is out there!

"I'm out of here!"

They headed for the door. The room was suddenly

empty. Three minutes later the night desk sgt., Shirley Kiser, came in, shook her head, and went to the desk. Marsh had left the usual note. "Have fun! Nick's on a case and we're out of here!"

<u>*Chapter one*</u>

Nick drove through the gates after arguing with the guard about not being on the guest list. The maid, a Lily White (*That* had to be an alias!), had neglected to tell them the cops were coming.

Nick told them the lab would be there soon, so don't obstruct them or they'd have "Tiny" Menthorne to deal with.

Anthony "Tiny" Menthorne was the only person Nick knew who was bigger than Paddy. Where Paddy was mostly just big, Tiny was big *and* obese!

You'd think a doctor would know better.

The front desk had taken over from Marsha to list everything they had. Nick was to go around to the right, along the service road, and into the rear entrance, where Lily White would meet him.

The body was at the rear stairs, which was why it seemed so strange to her.

As were most places at "The Pointe" (with an "E"), this was huge and ostentatious. Paradise Shores, more down to the south, was where the money-with-class set were located while "The Pointe" had the money-with-delusions set.

The Shores people were generally all right, from what contact Nick ever had with any of them, but these were a different sort. This wasn't going to be easy, no matter what. If it was only some older woman who fell down the stairs and died it would be touted as a cover-up. If it was murder it would be claimed the cops were trying to make headlines by making an accident look like murder.

"Damned if I do, damned if I don't!" Nick said as he got out of the car. "Where the hell is this Lily character?

"Wow! I'm already talking to myself!"

He shook his head, grinned, and rang the bell. An

attractive blonde girl in her early twenties opened the door and asked, "Yes?"

"Miss White? I'm Nick Storie, homicide."

"It's Mrs. Bad choice for names, hunh? Come on in. Nobody but me and Angie Kerr know about it, so try not to make a big stir?"

"If it's murder it won't be me making the stir."

She led him through a large kitchen into a short hall, where a dark, slightly plump girl was sitting on a chair by a door.

"This is Angela Kerr, better known as Angie. She's here from England, you know," Lily introduced. "This is Captain Storie, Angie.

"We locked the top door to the stairs from this side and one of us stays right here 'til you got here."

"I'm Lt. Nick Storie. Just Nick. Does the door open right onto the stairs?"

"There's a landing with a linen pantry toward one side and a little loo on the other, then the door," Angie said. "We knew not to touch anything, so I went up and clicked the lock with gloves. Fingerprints."

"Gloves? They'd erase prints, but there wouldn't be any on the lock lever. It wasn't used until you turned it."

"Those rubber things for handling dirty dishes," Lily said. "They won't erase anything."

Nick went into the small landing where the body was huddled at the base of the steps, asking Lily to watch for the lab van. He noted there was a door to either side of the stairs there and looked in to find shelves filled with canned goods and packaged foods in the one to the right and a large freezer in the one to the left. There was a pair of the latex gloves such as Angie had used in the freezer on a shelf inside the door. He quietly closed the door and moved up the stairs.

The woman was obviously dead. There was no need to check for vital signs with the head at that angle and the eyes wide and staring.

He noted everything as he passed and immediately concluded it was definitely murder. There wasn't much doubt to anyone with much experience with bodies.

The upper landing area was exactly as described by Angie. There weren't going to be any obvious clues left there. Nick could be certain of that!

Next step was to diagram everything there. The rooms, stairs, doors, light fixtures – everything. Nick didn't miss much.

He went back down as "Frog" Forest came in with his cameras. He was the photographer for Tiny's crew and would be even more thorough than Nick. He'd get every single inch of everything on videotape, then would take the stills.

Tiny was talking to the two maids, who were staring in open awe at the mountainous man. He saw Nick and waved. Nick pointed to the stairs.

"What?" Tiny asked.

"Woman, small, dark, about sixty, neck broken. She was dead when she went down the stairs. There won't be much in there. This one's definitely from scratch. I'll have to find out who knows something they shouldn't know or something.

"Lily, can you get a list of everyone here? Don't let anyone know anything's happening if you can help it."

"Uh-huh. I heard you say about somebody knowing something they shouldn't, you know. I'll get a list from the gate crew. It'll have most of them."

"It'll have *all* of them!" Tiny snorted. "Couple of asses at that gate! Idiots!

"You found something already, Nickie! I can tell!

Give!"

"Her head's lolled to the side."

"And?"

"Eyes wide open."

Tiny grunted and scanned around the kitchen. Angie and Lily looked expectant.

"No noise when it happened?" Tiny asked, looking at Angie.

"Lily heard a sort of thump earlier. About ten to six, but we were setting up the glasses and didn't check," Angie answered. "There's deep pile rugs on the stairs, so it might have been her body hitting the bottom. We wouldn't've heard bouncing on the steps, you see. The rugs."

"No outcry?" Nick asked (He tended to take on speech patterns of people he was talking to. He didn't realize it).

"We didn't hear, no."

"Karate chop and push," Tiny suggested, wandering toward the stairs. Frog came out and said for the crew to go ahead, but that place was clean.

"Did you get all four side rooms, top and bottom?" Nick asked.

"Hmm. Every inch," Frog said. "I'll get the other side of the upper door after Tiny okay's it.

"Freezer's interesting. In back, there're boxes of lobster tails."

Nick noted the look on Frog's face, nodded, and sat at the large square table to make some notes and diagrams. He heard a scooter outside, frowned, and stood as Lily came in.

"I got the list from the gateman. Barney asked what was going on, you know, and I said you got a tip about drugs. There's been some stink ... I should shut up. Here's the list."

Nick thanked her and sat with the list. It was names and times of arrival, who was in the car, and the license numbers of the cars.

Nick noted something was left out of the list, so called Frog over and asked a favor. Frog grinned and went outside.

"Is everyone here on the list other than the house's residents and staff?" Nick asked Lily.

"Even the staff. I think someone came on a boat. Maybe a couple. They wouldn't be on the list."

"That's what I was afraid of," Nick mumbled. "One of the umpty dozen things."

"We're just about through in here," Tiny announced, coming from the stairway door. "We'll take the body unless you say not to."

"Who was she?" Nick asked Lily. "We have to talk with next of kin first, if she had any here."

"Oh! She's Mrs. Sara Jane Johns! She's the one who owns this place on the deed, you know! Her son mostly sort of lives here, but he actually owns it. She's legal owner on paper, sort of, you know. Taxes or something."

"The son is here? Could you bring him in? Very quietly?"

Lily went out the door to the dining area.

So. Maybe this wouldn't be so difficult, after all!


"Mr. Johns? I'm Nick Storie. Homicide. I'm sorry to have to ask you to identify a body. I'm afraid it's your mother."

"HOMICIDE!? What the hell are you talking about!? MOM?!" Johns exploded.

Johns was a sort of flabby, dumpy, prematurely balding man in his early thrities. He had colorless hair and eyes, but there was a certain shrewdness about him that repelled Nick.

"Homicide's required to investigate all deaths in the home when a doctor isn't in attendance – and quite a few where there *is* a doctor present. I know this is distasteful and difficult, but it has to be done."

"Why wasn't I told?!" Johns demanded. "I won't have *anything* happening in this house I don't know about! Who called you before they told me?

"Little Lily and dear Angie! You're both *fired*! Get out of my house! I mean right now!"

"Mr. Johns, I suggest you show a little respect for the dead, particularly seeing as she's your own mother!" Angie snarled. "I worked for *her*, and wouldn't stay for such as you for any amount of money!

"You certainly are acting strangely for a person who's just been informed his *mother* is dead!"

"I ain't staying around here either, no matter what!" Lily threw in. "All that *drug* stuff, I can live without, you know!

"Maybe we didn't want your *guests* out there to be pulled into anything, but that was for *her! Not you*!

"You owe me two weeks, then I'm *out* of here!"

"Er, I didn't mean for ... I'm upset! Let's not start fighting here! I apologize. It's the shock. I never could face a crisis without losing my head.

"I'm sorry. Please! Wait until tomorrow when we're settled down, then we'll talk!" Johns cried as a very attractive woman in a tight white sheath gown opened the door to ask why Johns left his party like that. She noticed the police badges and suddenly looked shocked and a little frightened. She asked Johns what was going on.

"They say that Mom's dead!" Johns cried. "They're

*homicide*! She was murdered!"

Nick noticed his eyes weren't telling the same tale his manner was trying to get across. It seemed a little artificial to him. Johns was anything but shocked, and he certainly hadn't lost his head in any way. It was an act.

Maybe he was a bit scared – starting when Lily mentioned drugs. Nick wanted to know where Johns got his money.

"Ah-hah! Nobody said anything about any murder!" Lily cried triumphantly. "Maybe Detective Storie might like to know why you think she was murdered when nobody said anything about any murder before!"

"The bunch of you are real winners in a crisis, aren't you?" the woman said. "Detective Storie? I'm Emily Johns, wife to the headless wonder here. What happened?"

"A body, believed to be that of a Mrs. Sara Johns, was earlier discovered at the base of the stairs in there," Nick said. "Mrs. White called us and requested we come to the back quietly, as there was a party in progress and she wanted to avoid disrupting things if there was no cause to do so.

"You didn't notice Mrs. Johns wasn't present at the party?"

"Mother Sara wouldn't come until after the cocktails. She was against drink. I thought it strange she wasn't there to greet arrivals, but not excessively strange. She was likely to be late to such things.

"Why would she be on the back stairs?"

"Pardon me? Mrs. White mentioned that was rather strange. Why wouldn't she be back here?"

"Her arthritis. Those stairs are steep, so she used the front when she was walking all right or the lift when she was hurting. She never used the rear stairs. There's a small toilet on the upper landing, but she wouldn't use it. It's there for the staff. She would call if she wanted fresh towels or anything. She wouldn't go after them.

"She wouldn't be back there. Period.

"So! It *was* murder, wasn't it?"

"We'll have to get our reports, but I tend to think so. We'll have to ask some questions and look around.

"Other than in this area, which was in the province of Mrs. White and Mrs. Kerr, we have no authority, at the moment. Do I have to get warrants after we prove it was murder or can we go ahead?"

She smiled at him. "I like you! No bull, just say it!

"You have the freedom of the whole place. Anywhere. You don't need any warrants."

"Like bloody *Hell* they don't!" Johns snapped. "No bunch of cops are going to be running around *my* place!"

"This place belongs to the late Mrs. Sara Johns," Nick replied calmly. "Until the will is probated, it isn't yours. If we show she was murdered – and we *will* – we can get a warrant and can take this place apart. That warrant will read `The property and environs of *Sara* Johns.'

"Capich?"

"I'm as much an owner as he is and I give full permission," Emily said sharply. "Ben, they can take the place apart or they can do their jobs with a minimum of trouble. Stop being an ass!

"Detective Storie, do what you have to. Please try to keep interference with our guests to a minimum?"

"I have the gate list, so I'll only have to ask six or seven people if they heard or saw anything. The ones here before ten to six and anyone not on the list are all I have to question."

"Who wouldn't be on the damned gatemen's list?"

Johns demanded acidly.

"Anyone who came by boat as well as anyone who was here at the house before the list started. Would you please cooperate with Dr. Menthorne? Identify the body and allow him to remove her?"

"I'll identify, but you will *not* take her out and cut her up!"

"Ben! Stop being a total ass! You're making yourself look stupid! There's absolutely nothing you can do to prevent an autopsy under these conditions! Stop it!" Emily ordered sharply.

Johns' eyes were still telling Nick the real reactions.

"Oh, we're used to people's reactions to this kind of thing. We don't draw any solid conclusions as to intelligence from the way people act at these times."

He slightly stressed "act" and met Johns' eyes. Johns broke the gaze after a few seconds and went with Tiny. Emily looked a bit amused at Nick and shrugged.

"You don't quite fit here," Nick explained. "It's like you're from one world, he's from another, and the women working here are from a third. Strange."

"I didn't know what I was getting into when I married him. I wanted money and he said I gave him class.

"I am fond of him. Sometimes I hate him.

"To tell the truth, I always got along with Sara better than with him. There's something cold in him, Nick. I doubt he actually feels anything. He has to be very careful to project any emotions, but he doesn't experience them, so he doesn't get it quite right, if you notice. He'll yell and maybe even cry now, but watch his eyes. It's all an act.

"You already know that, don't you? That was what that little confrontation was about a minute ago. You won a round there."

Tiny and two officers took a Gurney out. Frog wandered in from outside and nodded shortly at Nick. Johns came back in and ambled around aimlessly for a few minutes, then suggested he'd better go prepare the guests for some unpleasantness.

"I'll handle it," Emily said. "Don't be vulgar, Ben. Don't say anything to the guests. I'll go after whichever ones Detective Storie has to talk to. We have to be discreet in these unpleasant situations."

"I'll first take Mrs. White's statement, then move on to Mrs. Kerr's, I'll have Lily come to you to tell you which people I have to speak to, if that's agreeable?"

"None of it's agreeable. We do what we have to. We try to maintain a certain grace with it."

She and Johns went out. "Oh! You aren't going to question *him*?!" Lily demanded.

"You can bet I will. Very long – and very intensely!" Nick grinned. "They way I work, I want to get some information first, so I know what to question him *about*! and how to phraase it"

"I see! How clever!" Angie remarked. "Don't go into battle without ammunition, as it were."

The door opened and a man in his late twenties slipped in. He was tall, dark, and powerfully built, with rather long dark brown hair. He looked back outside, then turned to grin at Lily and Angie.

"Right on schedule – for me! What the hell! Better late than never!"

"Nick Storie, Dan Carver," Lily introduced. "I don't suppose they particularly even noticed, Mr. Carver. There are forty eight people out there, other than the regular group."

Carver went to the doorway to the stairs, threw it open, and started to put his coat on a hook on the back of the door, then he glanced at the foot of the stairs and let the coat slip to the floor.

"Something wrong, Mr. Carver?" Nick asked.

"Is that some kind of sick joke? That tape outline on the floor. Is that supposed to be funny?

Chapter two

"According to the guest list you arrived at a quarter to six, Mrs. Billings?" Nick asked.

"I would think just about then.

"Officer, whatever's happened here? We understand Mrs. Johns, the elder one, is dead? An accident?

"Why the questions for an accident?"

"Routine procedure in cases where an unexpected death occurs and there's no doctor present. Until the coroner's court rules it's officially an unexplained death, regardless of what we think, personally.

"That rule was made to prevent any corrupt officer *or other* from hiding a crime.

"Was there anyone else here when you arrived, other than the Nesmiths and the people who live here and staff?"

"Well now, I noticed Angie, the kitchen maid. There were Mr. Clark and Mrs. Benson – Mrs. Benson was leaving. Her duties end at six, I believe.

"Ben and Emily and Shelly were in the atrium and came out when we came in. Connie came down from upstairs a few minutes later with David and Bart.

"There was a boat – other than the two Ben has – at the dock, but I don't know who came in it. It isn't one I am familiar with. I may have seen it somewhere, but wouldn't note ... that one."

"Arnold and Virginia Barnes, probably. They came by boat. I've spoken with them, but they say they didn't arrive until about five 'til six."

"No, no. It was one of those little bay boats, not Ginnie's Hastings," Phil Billings put in. "Ginnie has a forty two footer. A Hastings. That was one of those Cris Craft speedboats. More that type. Maybe eighteen – twenty footer. Dark brown, while Ginnie's is white. Not the same at all.

"No! Wasn't Ginnie at all! Little job! She has the Hastings!"

Nick didn't want him started again, so quickly said, "I see. No one else you saw?"

"Humph! That gigolo-type hanger-on or whatever was out back! Saw his back, but can't miss that one! Damned gigolo is all he is! Don't see what he wants here, but face it! Johns family aren't known for discretion!

"Ben and that bunch, that is. Don't know why Em ever got tied up with that bunch! She's way too good for the best of them!

"Sara was alright. She didn't put on airs and pretend to be what she wasn't. She was more to be proud of than the whole rest of them! Humph!

"Not Em, I mean. She was the only one of the bunch with any real culture. Only one!"

"Phil! We do *not* gossip!" Mrs. Billing ordered. "You are to stop drinking that champagne, and you are to stop with your incessant blathering!

"I'm sorry, Officer. He can't hold his liquor very well. We usually leave before he's had so much, but the delay of...."

"I understand," Nick said, consulting what he had written on his chart. "I have to watch it, myself.

"Angie Kerr, the maid. Mr. Clark, the houseman. Mrs. Benson, the housekeeper. Ben and Emily Johns. Shelly Johns, Ben's sister. Connie Terrell, Mrs. Johns' sister. Bart Fields and David Larson, house guests.

"Those were all you saw?"

"Ha! They're both damned cheap gigolos!" Phil retorted. "House guests my left foot! They're a couple of cheap gigolos! That's the type that whole Johns family are! Cheap trash!

"Except for Emily. She's alright. Only one with any culture whatever.

"Sara was alright. Didn't put on airs."

"That's all," Mrs. Billings said, glaring at Phil. "Is that all?"

"Yes. Thank you. I'm sorry for the inconvenience," She shoved Phil toward the door.

So. That's pretty much how Nick had it figured all along after meeting the whole bunch at the house.

Lovely people.

Nick went to the door and asked Emily to send in the Parks.


Nick deliberately waited until things settled down again. He interviewed all the suspects who were at the place before six, then looked over the list Frog got for him. That was something the gatemen overlooked. They took the license plate numbers and the people arriving in those cars – with the exceptions of the nine chauffeurs. He would have to check, but expected nothing.

The party was breaking up, Angie and Lily were in the great room picking up the glasses and dishes, and no one was in the kitchen, so he slipped into the walk-in freezer to see what Frog had found in back behind the lobster tails. He noted the rubber gloves were gone, but didn't think Tiny would find anything on them – then again, Tiny often found much more than anyone ever suspected he might.

The lobster was packed in four square boxes of twenty four tails apiece. That must have cost a bundle! Nick noted that they came from some company in Honduras. Rotan.

The boxes looked awfully large for only twenty four tails, so he opened one to look in.

They were huge!

Nick shook his head and slid the boxes out and onto the floor. Each box weighed more than a hundred pounds.

There were several sacks of white powder between the boxes and the rear wall. Nick untied the twist-tie from one and put a few grains of the fine powder on his tongue. His tongue went numb almost immediately.

So! Lily had said something about drugs – and here they were! *very* high-grade stuff!

Nick knew Frog had pictures of those seven sacks, so he slid one out and worked it into his jacket pocket where it wouldn't be noticed. He then slipped the lobster crates back into place and started making a careful diagram of the freezer. The door opened and Dan Carver did a double-take at seeing him there, grinned, and said, "Ha! I told them to always check this cooler before they hang the lock on the door!

"Aren't you glad I did?"

"I'm almost through. I have to make a list of every-thing here. The door opens almost against where the body was laying."

"You have to check the freezer? What? Looking for another body behind the beef?"

"We have to check this entire house, but the closer areas come first. I'm almost through in here. I've done the canned food pantry. Next is the upstairs, then all the rooms up there.

"She was killed at the top of the stairs, then shoved down."

"Killed ... then shoved down? Don't you mean shoved down and killed?"

"Oh, no! She was dead or as good as before she was pushed. Well! Now for the upstairs!"

He went out. Carver hung the padlock through the door handle, then waved, slipped on his coat, and went out the back door.

Nick pointed his finger at the closing door and said, "Bang!" Very quietly.

There was nothing to be found upstairs. Emily came out in a silk bathrobe around two thirty AM, looked surprised at seeing him checking the front stairs, and asked, "Detective Storie, when do you sleep? I thought you left hours ago!"

"Oh, I'm night shift. I try not to disturb people while I poke around. I usually get off work before now.

"There's not much here, I'm afraid."

"I can't sleep. Care for coffee before you go?"

Nick nodded and followed her down the stairs. She went to the kitchen and put some coffee in the Mr. Coffee, then sat.

"Are you married, Detective Storie?"

"Call me Nick. No. Next month."

"I'm not making a pass. I'm tempted at times, but that's one area Ben handles well. He has to. He has no emotions, so he concentrates on his bedroom technique. Surprisingly, he's an amazingly good lover.

"Do I shock you?"

"No. You don't fool around? Ever? With anyone?"

"Now I have to wonder if *you* are making a pass!" She laughed. "No. I'm afraid some great-looking guy like you would only disappoint me. My example is Ben, who isn't much to look at, but ... well!"

She got up and poured them each a cup of coffee, then got the sugar and cream to sit on the table. Nick tasted the coffee and sat back.

"I think you'll solve this thing, won't you?" Emily said, watching him. "You taste the coffee before pouring a lot of stuff into it to hide the flavor.

"It really is good, isn't it?"

"Mint and something."

"I read mysteries. There was something about mint and vanilla in gourmet coffee in one of them, so I tried it.

"It works if you don't overdo. Most people have no conception of what the words 'hint of' mean.

"Now! We've finished with the obligatory small talk, so you can tell me who did it. I assure you, it wasn't me!

"Do you have any ideas, Nick? Did Ben knock her off?"

"You think he's capable?"

"No. He wouldn't bat an eye about hiring someone, though. He would know who. He's had contact with that sort."

"Do you know about the drugs?"

"The stories about drugs? Yes. To be perfectly honest about it, I have no idea if any of it's true. I think Sara knew. I think it scared her, so I have to assume it's how Ben got his money. The real estate company and those pawn shops certainly can't explain how much he has."

"No drugs anymore?"

There was a slight noise from the back stairs. The door opened and Ben stood there.

"I thought you'd be down here, Em. Well now Storie! Skulking around with the wife at three AM?"

"I finished with the skulking about half an hour ago. We were discussing the drug business.

"I don't care about old history. You've been here for several years and limitations would probably protect you, anyhow.

"How did you make your money, Mr. Johns? Your wife tells me she doesn't really know, but she thinks maybe your mother did. There's not enough in your businesses to explain much of it."

"As you say, limitations would make it unnecessary for me to kill her. I made one hell of a lot of money *laundering* drug money. I never dealt with any drugs directly. It's too risky. I would never have gotten involved with even that if I'd known what was going on, but I was in it before I knew and couldn't get out.

"You know how that works.

"There's been nothing like that for years. I've retired.

"You see, Lt. Storie, there *is* a way out, but it's very risky. Damned dangerous."

"You have the proof, and they'd better back off?"

Johns made a wry face and shrugged.

"Well, Nick? Do you have any suspects yet?" Emily asked.

"I think I know who killed her, I just have to find some way to prove it. I'm stuck with several motives, none of which make any sense.

"I really have five or six suspects, but I'm personally sure who it was."

"Maybe we can help?"

"No. I can't concentrate on any one of them until I have a lot more. If I do that I end up missing the thing that would get a conviction of the real killer if I'm wrong.

"Did either of you see anyone around before the guests arrived other than the staff, your brothers and sisters and their lovers, the Billings, Barnes, Nesmiths, or Parks? I mean, before six or six fifteen?"

"Parks? Did they get here ... before?" Emily asked. "I didn't see them until right at six, when I came down to start greeting people. The others were in the great room.

"Wouldn't it logically be one of the people who live here?"

"Why in the hell would any of us kill Mom?!" Ben demanded. "Christ almighty! Why would any of us kill her?"

"Maybe she knew too much?"

"Then she'd have known it all along! That doesn't make any sense, but nothing else does, either."

"Well, I think you'll find the killer at the same time you find the motive," Emily said. "Maybe there's a little something around here somewhere that'll tie it all together, somehow.

"I know your team searched her rooms. I suppose you did, too?"

"I looked them over. It can wait until morning, so I'll come back with the crew and we'll do a much more minute search of the areas we think might be important.

"Her room and those at the top and bottom of the stairs are important, so we'll cover every inch.

"Who has keys to the rear stairway doors and to the pantry and freezer locks? Beside you?"

"The housekeeper and butler. We keep extra keys to the stairway door – top and bottom take the same key – in the table under the mirror in the upstairs hall, though I've never seen those doors locked.

"The key to the freezer is in the silverware cabinet. Only the staff know it's there."

"Could you lock the upstairs stairway door and take the key into your room with you tonight? I'll lock the freezer padlock and take the key with me.

"You have another?"

"There're spare keys to everything in my den," Ben answered. "Should I put them all in the safe?"

"For tonight, I'd appreciate it."

"You'll take the freezer key? Why? What did you find there?" Emily asked.

"For one thing, a pair of yellow latex gloves."

"I don't see how.... Oh! There were no fingerprints, and one doesn't leave rubber gloves in a freezer where they'll get brittle, so the killer put them there after he killed her.

"Nick, you're very intelligent, aren't you? I think maybe you *will* solve this one!"

Chapter three

"What do you have so far?" Paddy asked when Nick came in at nine the following morning.

"Nothing that I can realistically hope to bring into a court, really. I've got about enough to start my box chart. A lot depends on what Tiny has to report, but I tend to think there isn't much there."

Dr. David Klein, Tiny's assistant, came in with Marsha just then. He had a thick folder.

"Pretty much what Tiny said you'd decided before he got there to confirm it. Karate chop to the throat, then pushed down the stairs."

"What about the gloves? Anything?"

"What gloves?"

"A pair of latex gloves in the walk-in freezer. On the right, second shelf from the floor as you enter maybe three inches from the wall."

"Nothing about them," Klein said, searching through the report file. He picked up the phone and punched for Tiny's home phone. When he got a reply he asked about the gloves.

"He says Frog got the video and he checked them there, but they were clean. Not even body oil inside. He left them for the general inventory you'll take this morning."

"They're gone. Very interesting. If there wasn't any-thing in them, why were they taken?"

"Maybe the killer *thought* there was something in them?" Marsha suggested. "If they're gone and you know about it, they had to be taken before you left last night. The killer had access to the freezer after Tiny was there and before you left, so that should narrow the field."

"Oh, he had plenty of opportunity while I was talking

to the early guests. I just wonder why he took them at all. That's a lot more telling than ... something."

"Damn you, Nick! You already know who killed her, don't you?" Paddy demanded. "You always do this to me! Some stupid little thing gives it away and you can't ever seem to find the motive or something for weeks!

"Damn it! Who did it, and why?"

"A man called Dan Carver did it, but I don't have a tiny clue as to why. It may have had something to do with the drugs Frog found."

"Frog didn't report he found any damned drugs! What's going on?" Klein yelled.

"He didn't know they were drugs for certain. He told me he found something odd and where to look, so I looked. I left the sample in the evidence box, all neatly labeled – with the forms and everything. Didn't you check it out?"

Klein sighed heavily and picked up the phone as Marsh brought them each a cup of coffee. Jim Hill, the daytime homicide cop, came in and waved, then went to his desk.

Klein talked a minute, then held the phone, then said to call as soon as they had anything definite.

"Rookie. Didn't check the box," Klein said. "My fault. It's my job to check it first thing. Kid says its about two kilos of what looks like very pure coke. He'll run a check and report back."

"What? There were two kilos of processed cocaine hidden in that freezer?" Paddy asked.

"No. There were fourteen if that bag was two. I think the old lady found it and faced either Ben Johns ... oh, shit! I may be barking up entirely the wrong tree!"

"Don't do this to me!" Paddy cried. "What?"

"Maybe it was one or more of them? The gigolos? I

still have too many loose ends.

"I'll make my chart and see what I don't know. I'm sure Carver did it, but I don't know which one of them might have hired him. I'll have to trace the drugs.

"Lord! Don't let it be more than one of them! That, I don't need!"

"Why do you know it was this Carver person?" Marsha asked.

"Because a drunk saw him earlier from the rear. He said he was nothing but a gigolo, so it could have been one of two others, but he also said it was 'that gigolo-type hanger-on' – who could only be Carver. He spoke of the other gigolos as being part of the family, and they were inside with others at the time, leaving only Carver to be described like that.

"He's a physical therapist or diet workout instructor – or claims to be.

"I'll make the chart."

He went to his desk, took out a piece of construction paper, and divided it into a lot of squares. He filled in the times and places each of his major suspects were known to be at a specific location. He added what they were doing there if he knew. The end result being always that the killer was with the victim at the moment of the crime. The other information explained motive and method.

It almost always worked. Making the box chart kept him from forgetting little things. Little things generally solved the case.

Far too many boxes were empty when Marsha called Klein to the phone. He listened a moment, then put the receiver back down and reported, "Coke and opium, fifty-fifty. It was the purest we've ever tested. That little two kilo bag was worth on the order of half a million bucks by the time it reached the street.

"You say there were six more? Three million bucks? That seems substantial as a motive, wouldn't you say?"

"If we can tie it to anyone there. Any prints anywhere around the bag?

"Uh-oh!"

"The gloves were there for handling the stuff," Marsha suggested with a smirk. "They were taken to keep you from looking for what they were in there for. They didn't have anything to do with the murder."

"I don't know. Maybe they were removed for both reasons."

"There were two perfect thumb prints inside the bag," Klein said sourly. "The kid is sending them to Washington. He's also running a local check.

"They won't be the murderer. He wasn't there when they filled the bags. Those prints were from whoever held the bag open while the stuff was poured in. The flunky on this end wiped the bags clean, but he didn't wipe the inside of the bags. We'll find the same thing in all of them.

"You're sure they're still there?"

"If not we'll know who has them. I have one key and the other is in Ben Johns' safe. Anyone who wants in that freezer has to get a key from one of us."

"Ever heard of bolt cutters?" Klein asked.

"We'd have gotten a call by now if anything like that happened. I was never worried about that. If no one asked about the key and the stuff's gone it has to be Ben Johns. He can't let the key get away from him without Emily knowing, and she won't let anything get by her.

"Want to come along, Jim?"

"It's your case. I'm waiting for Ed Goins to call me. He's staking out a house where a guy who stabbed another guy is going to show up within the hour, so I have to be ready.

"Lonnie's coming out this Saturday. Marsha and Hank will be there. Shirley and Bill will be there.

"You coming?"

Jim's place on a barrier island was their gathering place off-duty, so Nick said he and Janet would be there.

He got his car and headed for the Pointe. The lab crew van would follow in about half an hour.


"It seems you only left a few minutes ago," Emily greeted as Nick came in the back door.

"Yes. I'll stay on the case until I've done all I can. I see you're still here, Lily."

"Angie won't be back, but I agreed to stay on until Mrs. Johns can, like, get somebody else. Work's hard to find. Mr. Johns isn't so bad as he seemed last night, you know. It's old lady Benson who makes it so bad. Mrs. Johns told her she runs me off and she does her job and mine both, so now she just gives those, like, hard looks, you know.

"Silly old bitch!

"Can I get into the lockup now? I got to get stuff for lunch."

"The lab boys will be here in a few minutes. I'll have them get the freezer and pantry first.

"Who owns the brown boat at the dock?"

"Brown? I don't know of anyone...," Emily said and went out to look, then came back in to say it was Dan Carver's runabout.

"He seems to pretty much have the run of the place," Nick said as Lily handed him a cup of coffee. "You invite your hired help to parties like that shindig last night?"

"Dan? Was he here? Of course not! Ben lets him run around almost like family, and he's some kind of friend of Shelly and Bart.

"He was *not* invited to any party of mine!"

"He thinks he's god's gift, that one!" Lily said. "Thinks he can snap his fingers – with us women, you know. I guess a lot of women like the type."

"I try to be nice to him to avoid friction, but I don't care much for the way he keeps putting little suggestive bits into his conversation," Emily added. "He doesn't seem to realize when he's been cut down.

"I think he knows if he ever goes too far with me Ben will hire someone to beat holy living hell out of him, so he gets to a certain point and stops.

"I think Sara confronted him about the way he acts around me and scared him. She considered him vulgar and crass."

Nick nodded, then she grinned and added, "She knew Ben and the whole rest of the Johns family are vulgar and crass. She wanted me to teach them how to act."

"She's the only one of them who actually ever learned how to show any class, you know," Lily said. "She was really very nice."

"She didn't put on airs, if certain of your guests from last night can be believed."

"And that's at least half of it, isn't it?" Emily replied. "Here's your crew. I've told everyone here they're to cooperate, like it or not."

Klein came in with several people. Nick unlocked the freezer and pantry as soon as Emily unlocked the stairway doors. Nick got Klein aside and told him where to find the drugs, but Klein said Frog showed him the videos.

Nick told Klein what to do after a few minutes, then

went into the dining hall while the crew did their work, then on into the game room where Dan Carver and Bart Fields were playing pool.

"Storie, isn't it?" Fields asked. "Sleuthing, or would you like in the game?"

"I'm mostly getting out of the way while the crew goes over the kitchen area."

He waited until Carver was preparing to make his shot, and added, "It's going to be a mess in there. They'll have to take everything out of the freezer, then the pantry."

Carver dubbed the shot. Badly.

"Why in hell would they take the stuff out of the damned freezer?" he asked offhandedly, studying the lay of the table.

Bart lined up a double bank shot and made it, then made two more. Nick watched and complimented him on his skill. He missed a very difficult double bank and kiss shot, then Dan lined up a simple straight-in shot.

Just before he shot, Nick said, "Because the damned gloves are gone!"

Carver missed the shot and swore.

"Gloves?"

"There were a pair of latex dishwashing gloves in there when we first checked, then they were gone."

"So what? What's that supposed to mean?" Carver asked.

"I haven't the foggiest. It's one of those things. They were there, then they weren't, so it has to mean something – but what?"

"Maybe the girls moved them," Bart suggested. "No one would keep rubber gloves in the freezer. They'd get brittle and crack. Besides, who'd shove their hand into a frozen glove?"

"No. They didn't. It's just an odd inconsistency. They

weren't important until they were moved. We'd have simply noted they were there and moved on.

"Inconsistencies solve murder cases."

"I see. You've definitely decided that it was murder?" Bart asked, making another difficult shot. "Eight cross-corner off one rail.

"You wouldn't have even noticed the gloves if the killer had left them where they were?"

"It was definitely murder. If the gloves had been left alone we would've put something like `One pair yellow latex dishwashing gloves, second shelf right, by front wall.' It would probably have been the end of it. Now we have to wonder why the gloves were in there in the first place, then why they were moved, then what else is odd in or around that freezer."

Carver looked a bit sick. He took the rack and balls and set them up without saying anything.

"Why were you here last night, Mr. Carver?"

"What do you mean?"

"You are a physical therapist who works for the Johns. You were not invited to the party. You work until four thirty, yet you came here around five thirty, then again about seven thirty.

"Why?"

"Five thirty? I wasn't even here then! I don't know what you're talking about!"

"You were *seen* here a few minutes before six. You came into the kitchen making some kind of statement about `better late than never' about seven. I was there.

"Hunh-uh. In that case it was better never.

"What? You had to see if we'd found her – or was it something else?"

"I don't know what you're talking about!"

"I've heard that statement hundreds of times. It's almost never true.

"I have to tie it together. I promise you I will."

"Are you saying I killed Sara?! That's crazy! Why would I kill her? You're nuts!"

"That's all I need. Motive. I have to tie it together. I have everything I need but that."

"And some little shred of proof." Carver sneered.

Klein came to the door to announce, "Nick, you're not going to believe what we found in the freezer!"

"ha! Just so it's not another dead body!" Bart said, with feeling. "Detective Storie just accused Dan of killing Sara!"

"No, I didn't. He merely asked me if I was doing that. All I said was I needed motive to tie it up.

"Did you find a motive for me in there, Dave?"

"A couple million bucks motive enough for you?"

"Could be! Enjoy your game, Mr. Carver. I'll be getting back to the detective bit."

As Nick and Klein left the room, Bart was saying, "What? A couple million bucks? In the freezer?

"Damn! I wish I'd known *that*!"

"Well?" Klein asked.

"We have no proof and he knows it, so he'll brazen it out. We have to tie it. He's not getting away with this one!"

Chapter four

"Washington identified your druggie who held the bag for you," Marsha greeted as Nick went into the office after lunch. "DEA, not FBI. They'll want the evidence as soon as we can let them have it. They'll tag him.

"Name is Carlos "Chico" Aleman. Miami.

"Call DEA officer Harry Jessup. He'll wait for your okay to pick him up, but he has such a tight tail on him he'll be easy."

Nick poured a cup of hot coffee and sat at his desk with the report, then asked Marsha to call Jessup.

"Lt. Nick Storie here. You can pick up Chico Aleman anytime you like. I'll arrange to come to Miami to talk with him. I can bring part of the stuff we have with his prints and an affidavit we have the rest. Okay?"

"Call me to tell me which flight. I'll have a man meet you. You don't want to carry that kind of drugs around unescorted, and the airport bunch would probably get you with the dogs as soon as you light."

They exchanged a bit of information and Marsha held up a note. He took it and said, "Flight seven oh four at five fifteen?"

"I'll have a man there from the airport security. We always have a crew for the international flights, so he's handy."

That left Nick about three hours to rest a bit before getting the plane, so he went home.


Marsha and Paddy met him at the airport with a little locked box wrapped in a plain brown wrapper he could carry on as hand luggage. They stayed until he was aboard.

The flight was a bit rough in one spot when they crossed a cold front moving through, but wasn't bad. At the airport ramp he saw a rather nondescript type standing to one side with a sign that said "Storie", and went to him.

"I'm Gadsden. Al. That the stuff?"

"Stuff? It's some crud from the forensics lab in Naples.

"You got maybe an ID?"

Al grinned and handed him his ID folder, along with a note from Jessup. Nick handed him the package and asked, "How does it feel to hold two million bucks in your hands like that?"

"Dirty. I've held more. Lots more.

"I have some bad news, I'm afraid."

"Which is?"

"Chico gave his tail the slip."

"Crap! Couldn't Jessup call and keep me from coming over here?"

Al shrugged and led Nick to an old black Plymouth. They drove to the DEA offices and into the parking garage. Al had Nick keep his face hidden in a newspaper "Mainly to be sure no one makes you for a later finger."

"This thing looks like it wouldn't make it to the next block."

"Got an engine and steering that could run Indy OR the drags. It's also got a lot of armor here and there and the side windows are bullet proof."

"I could see they were thick plastic." Nick said, getting out. Al didn't say anything and took him directly to the elevator. They went up into the DEA offices where Al dropped the package on the desk in front of a big man who looked like a bulldog to Nick.

"Jessup – Storie," Al said. "I'm going after supper. Levitt and Morse are covering nine two two. Alanza's coming in on it, so the flight'll be clean."

Jessup grunted and studied Nick, who decided he'd

study him right back.

"You got quite a rep as a murder cop."

"I never heard of you until a few hours ago and didn't bother to check up on you. I don't really gave a damn one way or another."

Jessup exploded in a loud laugh that almost made Nick jump.

"We're going to get along! Call me Jess.

"I like people who aren't intimidated. I can trust them.

"What do you think of my man losing Chico?"

"I think it's rather unprofessional. I have some important questions to ask whoever sent that stuff to Naples for storage."

"Chico's a bracero for the jefe. Guy by the name of DeGulio. Lives down at Raton."

"You think maybe Chico went visiting? I may have heard of a DeGulio, but I'm not sure. Some kind of drug supplier or something. not my department."

"Fifty-fifty he's there. DeGulio's my major focus of attention."

"Give me some pictures and an address."

"You gonna drive in and request an audience?" He grinned sourly.

"Ever tried it?" Nick returned the grin.

Jessup laughed again and slapped the desk. "To tell the truth, no! If it works I owe you a steak dinner!"

Jessup went to a file cabinet, then back to his desk. He swung his computer around, slipped a 3.5" disk into the external drive, turned on the printer, and punched in some orders. The printer rolled out three color pictures of three men and one of a big house. It then printed out a sheet of information.

"That's Chico, DeGulio, and Edward Murray. Murray's sort of his general business manager. That's the house and some information on DeGulio.

"Chico's a runner and gofer, not even a captain. If he's there I'll be a little surprised."

"Ah! I won't! I know something."

Jessup tossed Nick a set of keys to a Pontiac Grand Am and said to try not to get it shot up much. It wasn't armored.

Nick saluted and went to the parking garage, found the blue Grand Am in slot 29, and headed down to Boca Raton. He stopped on the way for dinner and arrived at the house about eight. There were two guards at the gate, but it was open, so he waved as he drove in.

There were twelve assorted (from and old VW to a shiny new Lexus) cars there, so DeGulio was probably throwing a party. It seemed everyone was doing that lately.

Nick checked his pictures, then locked everything in the Grand Am and sauntered into the big carved double doors like he owned the place. There were twenty five or thirty people milling around with drinks in their hands, so he went to the bar and asked where DeGulio was.

"Who the hell are you? I never seen you before!" the bartender said. "What you want with the jefe?"

"I'm a cop. I want to talk to him about something.

"Is Chico here yet?"

"Yeah! And I'm Fidel Castro! What's your name?

"Which Chico? Half the crowd's called Chico!"

"I'm Nick. Nick Storie. Chico Aleman." Nick looked around the room, but there was no one who fit the pictures there.

"He came in I think. Kitchen. He ain't exactly a mixer with this crowd. Are you really a cop?

"That would be wild, I think. I don't know how the jefe

would act if one walked in here and asked to talk to him!

"Nah! Can't happen!

"The jefe's in the den. Right through there.

"Are you really a cop? If you are I'll take you in!"

"Lead on, James! I'm a cop!"

"I'm Jorge. I think I'll call that bluff! Come on!" the bartender said and left the bar with a woman holding a glass out to him. She looked exasperated, but was going behind the bar as Nick followed Jorge into the hall.

Jorge rapped on a door, heard somebody call, "Yeah?" and threw it open.

DeGulio was there with a woman and Chico. "A cop to see you," Jorge announced, and stood back to watch as DeGulio looked amused, the woman headed for the door, and Chico dropped his drink.

"Thanks, Jorge. Ah! I see you beat me here, Chico!

"I suppose I'll be some little part of what Chico was discussing, Mr. DeGulio. I'm Nick Storie – from Naples South Station."

"Jorge, get Mr. Storie a drink," DeGulio said. "Have a seat, Nick!

"May I call you Nick? Call me Pancho.

"It seems you've cost me a lot of money, Nick, but that's part of business. No hard feelings.

"What do you want?"

"I should take Chico back to Miami with me. Leaving his fingerprints on all that dope was worse than stupid. It had to cause big problems, sooner or later."

"You have no authority," Chico whined. "I know that much!"

"Shut up!" DeGulio ordered. "Nick's right! You're more than stupid.

"Chico's suddenly needed in other places and will be

leaving the country very shortly, so I'm afraid he can't go back with you.

"Anything else?"

"Look. I don't have anything to do with DEA except that we found the crap and it had fingerprints on it, so I came here.

"I need some information about a murderer. You'll have that information.

"The killer won't ever be of any use to you again. You know  damned well that whole bunch is going to be watched *very* closely from now until hell freezes over. If I force the issue with Johns I open a can of worms I don't want any part of.

"All I want to know is if only the one person is involved or if he was hired by one of the others."

DeGulio stared hard at Nick for a minute, then shook his head and grinned. "You have more guts...!" he finally exclaimed. "I think I like you! I really do think I like you!

"Johns used to do little favors for some very wealthy people. He got moderately rich from it and found a way out. I don't want that can opened, either. As you noted, a certain person is no longer of any use to me. As a matter of fact, I'll be safer and better off if that person ceases to be in a position where he can do me any damage. I've long known he's an inordinately stupid person who is prone to allow his mouthings to involve others in situations they have no desire to, shall we say, confront.

"I will assume you will agree to prosecute that person for murder and not for ... other possible charges? (Nick nodded.)

"I trust you. One may trust another if that other has honor and intestinal fortitude.

"The money you cost me was the money I would've

gotten from him. I don't think anything I ever had anything to do with is behind Sara's murder. There was no one else involved with these products there – and my great anger is because my products were ever there at all. That Lanier killed her is by far the more likely scenario. Because of anything to do with me or my alleged product is as unlikely. There's something else behind it, Nick. I swear!"

"Lanier?"

"Not everyone there is using his right name," DeGulio replied with a smirk.

Nick grinned and stood. "It'll take me about an hour and a half to get back to Miami. Maybe that's time for Chico to have made his final exit from this country?"

"Ample. Nick, I honestly hope you'll visit me again after this is finished. A social visit."

Nick smiled and raised an eyebrow. "I think we're not exactly compatible, socially. We travel in very different directions in life.

"Too bad. I think we would probably be good friends under other circumstances."

"So life's a bitch sometimes." DeGulio smiled.

Nick headed back to Miami. He was more than a little surprised at Pancho DeGulio. He was a totally unexpected kind of person.


"You owe me a steak dinner," Nick greeted as he tossed the keys to the Grand Am onto Jessup's desk. "Chico's out of this country by now. He won't be back. That's part of our understood deal."

"And your murder suspect won't tag DeGulio," Jessup replied.

"He couldn't. At least, not with anything that would stick. I think you already know one hell of a lot more about DeGulio than he ever could give you, anyhow.

"One thing I didn't agree not to mention is a name. Lanier."

"Carver. Set up to keep a close eye on Johns, who's managed to stay clean, so we do the same."

"Set up by?"

"Sort of a syndicate deal. We think he was looking for an in to Johns' money on the side. The syndicate was looking for a control mechanism with him. Tie-in was the pawn shops in New York. Lots of money laundered through those places."

"Buy high, sell low? A pawn shop would be the place to move a lot of money in either direction. It could fence things."

"It seems Johns' pawn shops got stuck with phony jewelry all the time. They still had loads of cash to buy things with. Things that didn't exist or things that got stolen, but that weren't insured.

"I give you a couple hundred grand, you buy, say, an emerald from me for one ninety grand, then the emerald suddenly ends up missing. I have a legitimate receipt for having ninety grand. The pawn shop eats a paper loss of ninety grand. The ten grand commission gets banked in the mess, and it's a done deal.

"That's one of a million scams.

"Guy finds an old oak table in his grandmother's attic when she dies. He sells the table to a pawn shop that deals in rare antiques for fifty grand. The pawn shop lists the table in its inventory, along with a hundred other pieces, and stores it in a warehouse to auction later, but the warehouse burns to the ground two days before the auction! Oh, sob! The insurance only covered eighty percent!

"One place did that. Not Johns."

"Not Johns?"

"He didn't deal with insurance fraud or any of that. Much too sharp. Too easy to get tripped up. He only dealt the money in circles and took his off the top."

"Well, it's still keeping the drugs in circulation, so we'll resist going into whether one method is more moral than another. Funny thing, I liked DeGulio, who makes no bones about what he is and does. I do *not* like Johns, who tries for some kind of moral code."

"DeGulio has a strict code of his own. It's based on a much different thing. He sees himself as helping his people. If Americans get hurt, that's tough shit. His people come first. Johns sets his actions on odds of being caught. He has no real morals."

"They're Americans in South and Central America as much as we are here. Maybe if more people realized that, the moral arguments wouldn't hold."

"Don't get idealistic on me! This is the real world. I deal with it every hour of every day!"

"So do I. We each have our way.

"I'll take a rain check on that steak. I have to get back."

Chapter five

"You went all the way over to Boca Raton and didn't bring back anything at all, didn't you?" Paddy accused.

"No. I only said that I didn't get what I went after. I got something important, I think.

"Carver's working for the dealers, but he's supposed to be watching Johns for them. He's decided to run something of his own on the side. DeGulio thinks he's trying to get his hands on the Johns money. The drugs were another deal of some sort. I think he was supposed to hold them for someone else and had put them in the freezer to hide them. Something happened and Sara Johns had to be gotten rid of fast.

"He didn't plan that. The drugs wouldn't have been there if he did. Those drugs ... holy damned hell!"

He grabbed the phone and called information, but couldn't get DeGulio's unlisted number, so he called Jessup, who gave it to him. He then called DeGulio's and waited until he came on the line.

"Nick? Did you really think I'd still be up at this ridiculous hour? What did you forget to ask me? Think I can guess?"

"How many were there supposed to be?"

"Eight. I wondered why you didn't ask that last night."

"So you wanted me to explain what happened to the missing part for you?"

"How do you figure?"

"You don't know if Lanier's knocking down or whether – what if she found it and had some put back as proof? One of those things where the family couldn't get involved with anything like that, so he'd better get rid of it and stay away or she'd take a chance?"

"You see my problem. Who can I trust? Whatever he tells me, I still have to wonder."

"He knows that."

"You do see my dilemma, I see. How do I stay out of it? He claims there's something somewhere. It's an insurance policy of sorts. It would pay off in case of any odd accidents."

"Will he put on pressure to force you to get him out of the other?"

"There's no way I can. He knows it. I don't worry about that, Nick. He's between you and me and can't see any way out. He might try to take me down simply because he can make a deal."

"Chico's gone?"

"He's taking a vacation in a resort area where there are some millions of people who look and talk much as he does."

"Then anything he says won't ever have any corroboration, will it? No deals. Not from me."

"You *don't* know much more than you *do* know. That's not the only place he can make trouble. Nick, if you like I'll take a chance and solve your problem with him, but it *will* be a big risk."

"I might do it anyway. I can be on a vacation of my own if anyone finds his insurance policy."

"No! I have to solve my part of it in my way, Pancho. That would leave it up in the air for me.

"Do you understand what I'm saying?"

"My friend, I really do. I think it's dumb and a waste, but you don't think I'm very smart in some things, either.

"We look on problems from differing points of view. What I feel is a simple and permanent solution you see as merely adding one more thing to a long list.

"The way I see your way, you never really solve anything. The problem's going to remain after you close your little file. My way, it's finished. Permanently!"

"It's not that I disagree with that very much in more ways than you could know, Pancho. I have to solve the puzzle to where I know. I see your way as simply transferring it from someone else to your own head.

"It's a pity we can't get together to argue philosophy for hours."

"Life's a bitch. So you won't have to call and wake me up again, Chicago, Detroit, and the rotten apple."

"Thanks, Pancho. Get some sleep. You live a hard life."

"To be quite truthful, I live one hell of an easy life. Crime pays very well, my friend.

"Take the very greatest care around that bunch. They play by very different rules than either of us."

He hung up and Nick sat back.

"I simply don't believe you!" Paddy declared. "You just had a nice friendly conversation with a major drug lord!

"What kind of deal have you made with him?"

"That I won't investigate the drug end of this mess unless it can't be avoided. That's Jessup's job."

Paddy threw his hands in the air and went into his office. Marsha toasted Nick with her coffee mug.

Nick took out his chart, studied it awhile, then said, "Marsh, I don't think this thing's going to help this time. There are just too many things involved and I keep getting in deeper and deeper.

"Everyone agrees with me that Carver killed her, but I still don't know why! None of it quite holds up."

"She found the drugs and confronted him at the top of those stairs and he dumped her. Why won't that work?"

"Because there's a bag of that super-high grade dope missing. It would be where we'd have to find it if she had it."

"He found it first."

"Then he'd tell DeGulio first thing. He might well end up dead if he can't produce that last bag and knows it, so he'd have already done it." Nick shook his head and made a face at his coffee cup. "DeGulio is still very worried about that missing bag. I think he's afraid maybe she found out about it a few days ago and Carver's in the middle of a deal for his own skin with the DEA."

"Could it be?"

"No way! Jessup would've stopped me from seeing DeGulio if that was the case. I might spook him. There's something going on that I haven't considered."

"So?"

Nick sighed heavily. "Get me info in Chicago, then I'll work on Detroit, then New York. It's going to be a matter of slowly collecting grains until I have a sandbox to play in."

"Nick?"

"Yo?"

"Knock it the hell off with the bad metaphors! You always miss!"

He grinned and picked up the phone for Marsha to connect him with the Chicago police internet line.

Four hours later and he knew damned little more than when he started. Nick was frustrated and dead tired. No one knew very much about Lanier/Carver other than he spent too much time around syndicate types, but not many higher-ups. He wasn't brilliant. In fact, most considered him a moron. He was vain and thought any woman would find him entirely irresistible. There was a chance he was now trying to play two different crime families against each other, but that was generally fatal.

Bart Fields was known in Chicago as a professional gigolo with a small gambling habit, but not anything significant.

David Larson was educated, but lazy. He liked to let women pay him to be around.

An interesting fact: Connie Terrell used to be married to a middling successful man in the Doniletti family in New York. She was mentioned because the Doniletti family was one of the two Lanier was playing against one another, the Farris group was the other.

It was possible Fields had a tie-in of sorts with the Farris group.

Marsha had listened and taken her own notes along with Nick. She grinned as she looked at his notes. "Carver's watching Johns, Fields is watching Carver, and Connie's watching them all."

"Everybody's watching everybody else, but no one ever sees anything!" Nick complained. "I get the feeling I've looked at everything and listened to everybody, but haven't managed to see something or hear something.

"Or something.

"I'm going to have to grab some sleep. I'm going home. I'll be in about six.

"Marsh, I know damned well Carver killd Sara Johns. I even think I'll be able to prove it soon enough, but I'm going to go nutzville if I don't figure what the *hell* this is all about! It's not possible it's as complicated as all this crap! Carver's too stupid for it to be anything like this!"

"Look at it from each separate angle as if that's the only thing. One of them's it. The others really *are* incidental."

"One: Sara found the drugs and confronted him. He had to stop her fast. That doesn't work because there's a bag of dope missing she didn't have.

"Two: She confronted him about something else and the drugs merely happened to be there. The fact those drugs are there and that Johns is who he is is why anything else happened. It isn't really related.

"Three: She didn't confront him. He lured her there to kill her for some reason.

"That doesn't work because he wouldn't do it if the drugs were there. He killed her on the spur of the moment. That's defin...."

"And you just grabbed the brass ring! Give!"

"Sara Johns had gone up the front stairs a few minutes before she ended up dead at the bottom of the rear stairs. She ended up dead at the bottom of those stairs because she was going up to her room and saw Carver up there! He was supposed to be gone, but he was up there!

"Lily and Angie were in the kitchen when she was pushed down the stairs, so he did *not* leave through the kitchen. There were guests at the bottom of the front stairs, so he did *not* leave by them.

"He was seen outside a few minutes later by Philip Billings.

"Either he didn't kill her – or he left through an upstairs window – or something. He couldn't have come from a front window because of those chauffeurs out there. He couldn't have come from in back because the Barnes were coming in from their boat and would have seen him. The only way he could have left was through the atrium, which has a trellis from the second floor to the ground anyone could use as a ladder.

"Shelly and Bart were in the atrium and would have seen him. He didn't kill her. My chart shows that fact pretty clearly. It does work after all, but now I'm really in for it."

"He killed her. You showed that when you confronted

him in the pool room. You have all that in your notes, and I typed it for you.

"Shelly and Bart left the atrium about five to six. Billings spotted him about then, so he waited until they left the atrium, climbed down fast and went out back.

"Sara was killed because of what she saw him doing when she went up."

"Or *where* she saw him. Maybe it's because of what she saw him doing in some specific place?

"Okay. What I'm going to do now is get some sleep and clean up, then go back out there and have a talk with people."

"Weren't that Connie character and her gigolo boyfriend up there?"

"They were in the game room – or they came from there. The stairs come down right by the door, so they could have walked through, but I think they were in the game room."

"You didn't search those rooms, except for Sara's?"

"No. There was no real reason to. I'll take a good look in all of them now. Maybe I'll spot something, but I won't have any idea what I'll be looking for, really."

"I'd say it's a bag of dope. The missing bag has to be behind it somehow. You don't have anything else that could connect things."

"Maybe, but I think maybe that's become secondary," Nick said, standing and stretching. "I think there's something else. I think Carver was up to something very different from the dope business.

"See you tomorrow!" He went out to his car and home.

Nick laid on the bed and thought about what different people had told him. It all held up very well in some ways, but didn't really tell him what he needed to know, and he wasn't going to figure it out like this. He'd have to make the connection when that certain little fact came home to roost.

He'd started out thinking Carver was pretty clever. He seemed to have covered his tracks very well. Now he thought Carver was a vain fool. It was purely stupid for him to have come in when he did parroting that stupid cliché about `Better late than never.' It was easy and obvious to find he wasn't invited to the party. The simple fact was, he'd be better never than late – to a party he wasn't supposed to attend in the first place. That was when Nick knew he was the killer. He'd let his curiosity get the best of him when there wasn't a huge stink and had to find out what was going on. Had he not come in at all Nick would probably never have connected Billings' statement about the gigolo hanger-on. He'd figure Billings meant either Bart or David, though he would have had to question how Billings saw him outside, when he had pretty well proved Bart and David were never out there.

Next, he had taken those gloves. There was nothing to connect the gloves to anything, but he took them, making them obvious.

Most telling about the idiot's IQ was when he pulled some kind of idiotic blackmail act with a drug lord like DeGulio. That was immensely stupid of him. It was tantamount to suicide. DeGulio had as much as offered to have him killed. Nick could take credit for Carver being alive right now. He'd asked DeGulio not to kill him as a more or less personal favor.

Maybe he was as stupid as Carver was, but he actually *did* like DeGulio! He was charming and he was a very intelligent person even if Nick thought that intelligence was misguided.

Like Pancho said, "Life's a bitch." Nick drifted off to sleep.

Chapter six

Nick hadn't ever considered the lift. He checked it over and decided it didn't figure because it was right beside the stairway and opened on the landing upstairs right beside where the stairs stopped. It might be important to know if it was up or down at six o'clock, but there wouldn't be any way to know.

Lily said Sara always used it when her arthritis was bothering her. It had been, so she'd used it.

Nick stepped inside and punched the up button. It operated silently, so she might have stepped out of it and seen ... what?

He slid the door open and looked down the hall. He could see the doors to the four rooms to his left and the two on the right farther down, then the door to the back stairway.

Looking back the other way he could see one door on his left, then the light from the open atrium with a door across from it on the right. There was a large fixed window at the end of the hall.

She could have seen anything.

Her room was first door to the right facing the rear stairway. Next was Connie's room, then the rear stairway. Across from the rear stairway was Larson's room, then Emily and Ben as you came back. Two doors. Then the door to a bathroom, then the door to Shelly's room, then the elevator, then going on down past, Bart's room, then two guest rooms.

Okay. Sara came up the lift, and saw Carver at the end toward the back stairs. She started toward him, he saw her and slipped into the rear stairway. She wanted to know what the hell he was doing and went back. He struck her across the throat and pushed her down the stairs, then stood a minute to see if anyone came from the kitchen.

He had on the gloves already. He didn't want to leave evidence he'd been there and knew someone would look for prints.

Whatever he was up there for, he didn't find it. Nobody looked for prints from any source other than the murder.

Okay. He went down, checked to make sure she was dead, and ditched the gloves inside the freezer so he wouldn't be noticed wearing them – stupid again, because it would be smarter to put them in a pocket and carry them out with him. He went down to the stairway door into the kitchen and could hear Angie and Lily in there working with the glasses at the table, so he went back upstairs. As soon as the coast was clear he headed for the front stairs, but there were people down there – and he *must* not be seen.

The atrium was obvious. He waited at the top in the hall until it was clear, climbed down the trellis, and went out the door. He was heading down to his boat when Billings saw him.

There was no uproar. A car came, a van, and even an ambulance, but none of them used emergency lights or sirens. From the water side he couldn't see much.

Then the EMS ambulance left, then the van, but the car stayed, so maybe that was a guest.

There was no big uproar! What if she wasn't dead?

He had to know. She had seen him very clearly. He went back in to find Nick at the kitchen table, so made an excuse for being late and went in to look for himself. Maybe nobody found Sara and the ambulance was for something else.

There was no body for him to "find," and he had to come up with another excuse, so pulled the bit about the chalk outline.

Nick went from the elevator to the rear stairway and in, stood for two minutes, went down and opened the door to the freezer, paused a few seconds, went back upstairs, opened the door with his handkerchief, walked along the hall to the atrium trellis, waited two more minutes, climbed down, and went around and down to the dock.

A little less than seven minutes. It could be done with two and a half minutes to spare.

Nick headed back up to the house to find Emily and Ben sitting on the little terrace watching him.

"You checked your watch, so who did it and how?" Emily asked.

"I won't say who, but the killer was doing something upstairs in the last two rooms on either side toward the rear stairway door. Sara went up in the lift, saw him, and went after him. He slipped into the stairway hall and she went in. He killed her, checked to be sure she was dead, heard the girls in the kitchen, went back upstairs and to the atrium, waited until no one was in the atrium, climbed down the trellis, and got out."

"I thought it had to be Carver."

"Don't let him know I've figured it this close," Nick requested seriously. "I've told him I know he did it. I did that yesterday.

"I have to get motive. He didn't really leave a clue I can take to court, so it's a matter of getting something or letting Pancho DeGulio get rid of him to close the case."

Ben dropped his orange juice. "DeGulio is behind it?!"

"Only because he thinks Lanier was pulling a double-cross with someone else with his ... product. A person like Pancho doesn't let loose ends flutter around."

"I always said ... Lanier? Oh, my god! Carver is Lanier? Mike Lanier?

"So. You found dope in the freezer. That's what that was all about. He's stupid enough to have hidden it there."

"You didn't know?"

"That he was Lanier? No. I know who Lanier is from his reputation and for who he works for."

"You can figure why he's here, then."

"So he can watch me and get me out of the way if they tell him to. That means he was probably searching my rooms for the evidence that keeps me out of their clutches.

"That doesn't make sense, except that Lanier would be far too stupid to realize it wouldn't be anyplace like in my room.

"Maybe not. Even *he's* not that stupid.

"I wonder what he was looking for."

"If I can discover that I'll have him dead-cold. If Lanier has that bad a reputation, why does anyone use him?

"I think he was watching you, but he was doing something on the side. Apparently, DeGulio was using him to deliver drugs."

"Come on! DeGulio wouldn't use anyone like him for anything!" Ben retorted. "You'll have to meet the jefe. He's very charming, in his own way. I think you'd like him because he's direct and honest. One thing he is definitely *not* is stupid! My personal opinion is that he's a bona fide genius! He'll use violence if he sees no other way, but he finds it much easier to move people around to a place where they can't do much damage ... so how do you know about him at all?

"You were able to trace drugs from Lanier to him?

"I don't think so! I really do *not* think so!"

"I did meet him, and I *do* like him. The drugs had

fingerprints we traced to a person who works for him. He wiped the bags carefully, but held them with his thumbs inside when they filled them, so we traced.

"He's gotten the fellow out of the country, so we can't get a legal connection between him and the stuff. He's the one who told me that Carver is Lanier. Pancho's worried about what Lanier was doing here besides the obvious surveillance. There's something missing, and he's very worried about where it might be and who might have it."

"Even *Lanier* is not stupid enough to second deal DeGulio," Ben protested. "*No*body's that stupid! If there's something missing, Lanier's looking for it, too. He's a dead man if he can't find it."

"Pancho's going to wait. Maybe I can find it and find out who was doing what to whom. I think Lanier made a bit of a threat to Pancho. I think he'd be smart to confess to killing Sara so we'd have the job of keeping him alive until the trial. If he does have anything he could make a fast deal for relocation with DEA."

"Right! The government can protect Lanier against DeGulio! DeGulio owns people in every prison in the southeast and probably more. You can't protect him. DeGulio can call in favors from every major syndicate in this and several other countries."

"Pancho said Lanier's between him and me and there's nowhere to turn. He agreed to wait, so I'm keeping Lanier alive at the moment.

"I think Pancho will keep his word about that, but he made it plain there's a time limit."

"Honestly! You amaze me!" Ben said, shaking his head. "You call him Pancho, and you've made a deal with him?

"You? A cop?

"His word's inviolable. If he said it he'll stick to it, no matter what.

"Would you tell me how you got to even talk to him in person?"

"I went to his house and asked the bartender to tell him I wanted a word. The bartender thought it was so cool a cop would come there he took me in. Pancho was amused. He said I was the first cop who ever did anything like that. He said I have guts. He respects me and I respect him. We have two very different philosophical perspectives, but we both have a strong code.

"I think I'm finally getting a small glimmer of what might have happened here. Is your offer still open for me to search things without a warrant?"

"Seeing as I don't have any secrets left anyhow, why not?" Ben grinned. "Em would tell me to shut up if I objected, anyhow."

"Did you know David Larson used to be tied up with Doniletti?"

Ben spilled his orange juice again, then shook his head. "You like doing that, don't you? You like to prove you can shock even people like me.

"No. He wouldn't be in my house if I'd known. Connie may be my aunt, but there are limits."

"She has connections, herself."

"Her marriage to that hood is what got me into it. I thought it was all behind us. I'll get that one out! Fast!"

"Make a deal like the one Pancho made with me?"

"Same deal. There's a time limit – and it's not a long way off. That means Lanier's working for Farris. They're watching each other *and* me! Know something, Nick? I think it's getting funny! It's like a bad TV show with too many heavies."

"Even better! They're trying to out-crook one another!"

"Does that mean you think the missing things from this Pancho DeGulio character was taken from Dan by David?" Em asked with a grin. "So now Dan's in trouble with DeGulio, but David can't do anything with what he has, because then DeGulio will come after *him*!"

"Even better!" Ben said. "Now David has to get rid of what he has, but he doesn't dare! If he's caught with it, Lanier knocks him over, but he'd *better* have it to give if DeGulio comes for it! No matter what, Lanier loses – and so does Larson!

"Your time limit just went a little longer, Nick!"

"They both had the job of watching you. Now they both have to spend their time watching each other and their own rears. Lanier isn't sure David has it. If he was David would be dead.

"I don't think he knows Larson's connected with that Doniletti crowd. I think maybe he's worried about Connie.

"Terrible communications, eh what?"

Emily giggled, then said, "It's still deadly dangerous to all of us, isn't it?"

"Make no mistake about that," Ben replied sharply. "Those type hoods only know one solution to any problem. You corner them and they'll come out killing. It won't ever register that a killing is what took a merely bad situation and made it an impossible one for all of them. When you consider how Lanier isn't exactly known for smarts anyhow, you see how bad it can get.

"I never thought I'd be glad a cop was hanging around. I don't know what you can do, if anything, but it's nice to know you're close.

"Is what's missing part of a drug shipment? Something some hood would figure on making a fast ten grand on?"

"Try two hundred grand."

Ben whistled. "Quality or quantity?"

"Mostly quality, but a little of both."

"Bring in dogs!" Emily suggested.

"I was planning to."

"We found a little pot residue somebody spilled at the party or something and one small cut of hash behind a sofa cushion," Joe Hardy, the dog expert said. "The dogs seemed to find that plant room interesting, but didn't give us a definite location. It could be something that's growing in there or it could be old traces. They went all over the place sniffing. They were acting like they wanted to point something out, but didn't know quite where."

"It's definitely not anywhere else?" Nick asked.

"Not on these grounds. I'll take the dogs back home. They've done all they can. The cars and boats are all squeaky clean."

Nick nodded and filled out his forms and signed them, then Joe took the dogs and left.

"Well, they didn't find it here, so it must be gone already," Emily suggested. "All the cars are here. So are the boats, so it must already be gone."

The whole bunch were standing around asking each other what the hell was going on. Dan Carver/Lanier was looking disgusted and a bit afraid, while David Larson was almost smirking.

"Oh, they found it. You can find a thing by eliminating locations until there's only the one left where it has to be."

"Oh? Where is it?" Larson asked.

"I only know it's here. The dogs told us that."

"Then whoever put it wherever it is will have to find it and move it before you find it!" Connie exclaimed. "All you have to do is watch for somebody to move it!"

Nick could have gleefully strangled her.

"Aunt Connie, you can be the stupidest one broad I've ever come across!" Ben snapped.

She looked confused, but it was an act. Nick could see a lot of Ben in her. She suspected David – or had it herself. That was still a possibility. This was the first big case he'd come across where he met so many people he disliked. Most cases he even became friends of sorts with the ones he caught.

Again, he thought of Pancho's little remark. "Life's a bitch!"

Chapter seven

Everyone had finally wandered away except Emily and Ben. Nick didn't think they were really involved to any great extent. Emily because she was smarter than that and Ben because he was clever and cunning, but not so smart. He'd had enough sense to know when he'd had enough, so he'd gotten out and intended to stay out.

Nick sighed heavily, went to the trellis, and began climbing, checking all along. He found it a few feet below the second floor on a support brace hidden by a thick Thunbergia vine.

"Mrs. Johns? Would you do me a favor?"

"Certainly."

"Call the department and tell them to send Frog and a man who can climb around in difficult circumstances."

"Is that a diplomatic way to tell them not to send us that huge mobile mountain who was here before? I take it you've found what you were after?"

"Yes. To both."

She went into the great room to call. Ben said he'd stay right there to keep Nick company until the police arrived.

Nick climbed down and stood with Ben and Emily, who'd come back to say the lab van would be there in about twenty minutes. She then took a compact walkie-talkie from her skirt pocket and asked Lily to bring them a pot of coffee and some cups.

Ben went into the great room for three chairs and a little end table and told Em some almond Danish with hot butter poured over them sounded good, so she ordered that.

Ben had placed the table to one side under a palm where they could see the spot the bag was hidden, but not the upstairs rail. Nick raised an eyebrow at him.

"I know the kind of people you're dealing with in this mess. It's best we're not sitting right out there in plain view. The old adage is that if you can see them they can probably see you. It's beyond question better if they can't see us.

"Are you armed, Nick?"

"Ben!" Emily cried.

"He's right," Nick said. "Lanier's desperate about now. So is friend Larson if his prints are on that bag. They're both in a position where there's no way out, so they might strike out at anything or anybody."

He took out his .32 and laid it on the table. Emily shuddered.

Lily brought the coffee and Danish. Nick suggested she sit with them, which Emily seemed to approve of but Ben didn't. He kept his silence.

"I have to finish the food," Lily said. "Why do you have that gun there?"

"Lily, you may be a lot safer here than alone for the next few minutes. Only until the crew gets here."

"Why? I don't know anything!"

"Because someone else may think you *do* know something," Emily said. "Lily, the person we're afraid of is very scared right now. He may think you heard or saw something when Sara was killed. You and Angela were through a thin door from where he committed a murder.

Lily's eyes flew opened and she paled. She shakily sat on the chair Ben brought from the other room.

There was the sound of a horn out back. Emily waved for them to stay seated and went out to bring Frog and Tiny in.

"There's no way you can climb up there!" Ben said to Tiny. "My god! That trellis won't hold that kind of weight!"

Tiny grinned and wiped his forehead with the towel he carried for that purpose. "Frog is an officer of the court and of the coroner's office as well as a licensed forensics expert and a deputy sheriff.

"What else can I tell you?"

Frog looked at Nick, who pointed to the spot where the bag was secreted. "It's on a brace behind that vine with the pale blue flowers. It could have some very important prints on it, okay? – and be careful. Watch for *anyone* who might come onto the rail above you. At least two people have already put their necks in a noose because of that bag."

Frog nodded, and started climbing the trellis with a camcorder strapped to his head. Emily watched him strap it on and shook her head.

"His own little invention," Tiny said. "He doesn't miss much."

"So. Why do you call him Frog?" Emily asked. "He'd actually be rather attractive if he cut his hair and wore decent clothes."

"I don't know. I never asked."

"That name was from biology class in high school," Nick replied. "They were to dissect frogs one day and he sneaked a live one into class, laid it out on the board, and called the teacher over to ask a question. The teacher started to instruct the students about making the primary incision and the frog started kicking. The teacher freaked out and Frog ended up in detention for two weeks. The other students started calling him "Frog Man" Forest, and the "Frog" part stuck."

Tiny shook his head. "Frog never ceases to amaze me with his expertise on almost any subject, and now you know more about the people in my department than I do!

"I begin to feel redundant and insignificant!"

"*You* will never be insignificant in any least sense!" Emily grinned. "Have a Danish? They're still warm.

"I don't think I want...!"

There was a loud, terrified scream from upstairs. Nick reacted without thought, grabbing his pistol and racing for the stairs. Frog, who was almost to the top of the trellis, swung up to the rail three feet above him and looked along the upstairs hall.

"Stay up there, Frog!" Tiny called. "Nick's going. You finish what you're doing!"

Frog shrugged and went back to remove the bag of dope after first taking several still shots with a flash camera.

Nick raced back, noting Shelly was opening the door of the bath into the main hall to look out. Bart was running down the hall, and Carver/Lanier was coming out of the rear stairway into the hall.

The door to Connie's room was open. There were sobs and moans coming from in there.

"Stay back!" Nick ordered and leaned low around the door to see Connie bending over David Larson. There was blood all over the place.

Nick slipped his pistol back into its holster and went in to pull Connie back. Larson's throat was slashed from one side to the other. There was a bright silver thin switchblade laying on the floor beside Larson's body.

"Tiny!" Nick yelled. "Call the full lab! Get up here!

"Frog! Take the evidence to the van and seal and lock it, then get up here! Fast!"

"Ambulance?" Tiny called.

"Wagon!" Nick called, then turned to the people gawking at the door. "Take Mrs. Terrell out and clean her up, will you Miss Johns?

"I'll want statements from all of you, so fix tightly in your minds where you exactly were and what you were doing during the last ten minutes. Clear?"

He waited until Tiny came in, then Frog a few minutes later, and went out to say, "In the atrium. All of you. No arguments!" He marched down the stairs.

"Well, you three are out of this one," he announced when he got back to the table.

"What's happened now? Did Lanier knock over Larson?" Ben asked with an almost amused look.

"Larson's definitely been knocked over, as you call it. You think Lanier killed him? Why?"

"I expected it. It's why I said I'd wait to throw him out. Steal the stuff from Lanier and he has a single response. That's it! You'll be able to tag him for this one, so he might as well confess about killing Mom.

"I'll be much damned gladder than you know for this to all be over!"

"You and me both!"

The two from upstairs came in together. Shelly and Connie were apparently still in the bath. Nick suggested they bring chairs in to sit around.

"I'll do this part a bit differently than I usually would," Nick said, sitting a small tape cassette recorder on the table. "Most cases I'd try to take you one at the time to trip you up. You haven't had time to fix any stories now unless somebody fixed one before Larson was killed.

"Mr. Fields, you first. Everything from the moment ten minutes before the scream."

"There's really nothing to tell. I was laying on the bed reading about Princess Di and Charles and how Elizabeth's handling her flaky family. It's in the `People' section of today's paper."

"No one was with you in that time?"

"No. Shell was in the bath washing her hair."

"The whole time?" Nick kept his eyes fixed firmly on Fields' face.

He paused to think a few seconds. "And about fifteen minutes before. I could hear the dryer for about six or eight minutes, I suppose. It's one of those old blower things. It whines."

"Thank you." Nick turned to Carver. "You?"

"I went to the kitchen for coffee. I don't go upstairs very often. As you said before, I work here. I'm not socially acceptable!"

"You seem to spend an inordinate amount of your time wandering around everywhere in this house. Getting into personalities here won't serve you very well. I'd think you'd want to make friends about now, not aggravate the situation.

"You weren't upstairs at all?"

"I was earlier, when you came. Hell! You *talked* to me up there!

"You asked about ten minutes before she yelled. I was down in the kitchen."

"Lily can confirm that, then."

"She wasn't there."

"Oh. Right! She was with us down here waiting for Frog and Tiny to come after the stash in the trellis."

Lanier stared at him, then shrugged. "That where he hid it? I sort of thought so when the dogs didn't find it."

"Pancho will be happy to know it's been located, I suppose. He was a tiny bit worried it might fall into the wrong hands."

That shook him! When Nick said "Pancho" Lanier looked like he'd been punched in the stomach. Hard. He was obviously much more scared now, too.

"Er, Pancho?" Lanier asked.

"Uh-huh. DeGulio. He was worried about the missing bag. He was afraid somebody might make the mistake of using it to threaten him."

Lanier looked very sick. "I'll make a deal! State attorney and DEA! Not you!"

"The evidence is already in our hands. We traced the stuff in the freezer to DeGulio, but he was covered for that. You don't have anything to deal *with*. Not now."

"What the hell is going on!?" Bart demanded.

"There were several kilos of pure drugs hidden in the freezer," Ben answered. "Lanier – that's Carver's real name – put them there. They didn't belong to Lanier, they belonged to a drug lord by the name of Francisco DeGulio. Lanier was supposed to deliver them to somebody, but didn't. Larson found the stash and took a bag. He was going to turn a fast buck or two. He had the connections to move it.

"Lanier was looking for the missing bag when Mom caught him, so he killed her. He wasn't quite sure it was Larson who had the stuff, but now Larson discovered who really owned the dope, so he was in a very tight spot. He didn't dare to get rid of it – but keeping it could be even worse.

"It was a sort of Mexican standoff. So long as no one knew where the bag was, Lanier didn't dare to kill him. He could stay alive, but only so long as the drugs were missing.

"Then Nick found the drugs. Lanier figured he was off the hook now, so he did what his type always does. He came out killing!

"He killed Mom, and made his situation go from simply bad to impossible. You'd think he'd learn, but no! He had to get revenge on Larson for taking the dope, so he killed him.

"His impossible situation, as could be expected, went from merely impossible to absolutely, hopelessly, ridiculously lost!

"You idiot punk! If Larson was alive he would have to take the heat from the jefe! Now it's *all* on your head!

"That how you see it, Nick?"

"Mostly. Now you have nowhere to turn, Lanier. If we can protect you maybe DeGulio won't kill you. Mrs. Johns wasn't first degree and no one would ever suggest the chair for killing a hood with a record like Larson had.

"I suppose you knew he was working for Doniletti?"

"That's where you're wrong! He was working for Tom Farris for the last few years. Doniletti has someone else handling that end."

"You?" Ben accused.

"I got nothing else to say to any of you!"

Shelly led a sobbing Connie in and sat her at the table. Jim Hill and Ed Goins, homicide cops, came in and Nick told them to take Lanier into custody, but to hang around for a few minutes.

"Miss Johns, I have to get a quick statement from you women. I'll take yours first, then Mrs. Terrell's.

"Tell me exactly what happened for the ten minutes preceding Mrs. Terrell's scream."

"We left you earlier, and went to my room – Bart and I. I decided to wash my hair. Bart was laying on the bed reading something.

"I washed my hair and rolled it up, then I was drying it and she screamed. I turned off the dryer and went out and you were coming up the stairs."

"I see. Thank you. Mrs. Terrell? I know this is difficult for you, but I have to take a statement while everything's fresh in your mind. The shock will make you block things later. What happened? Everything from when you left us here."

"I just can't.... It's so confused! We came up, Dave and me. Dan went back toward the pool room or something and Shell and Bart went up ahead of us. We said we'd take the boat out later, if things settled down a bit. We have to get out of here for awhile!

"Let me think ... we went to my room and talked about what happened and wondered what you were looking for. Dave said it was obviously drugs because of the dogs, but he said he knew for a fact that Ben wasn't involved in that kind of stuff anymore. We talked! We didn't *do* anything, or anything.

"I had to use the bathroom. I went in and came out and there he was! I wasn't gone more than a minute! It couldn't have been even that long, because I just got in there and remembered my book was on the night stand – I read while.... Oh, my god! I can't stand this!"

"You weren't out of the room for more than, say, two minutes?"

"It wasn't even *one* minute! I went out again as soon as I saw my book wasn't in there! It wasn't even *one* whole minute! Maybe about half a minute!"

"The door was open?"

"The door? What...? But ... but ... we never closed the door! It was open all the time!"

"Thank you. Mrs. Johns, I'm sure Tiny will give you a sedative for Mrs. Terrell. She's had a severe shock."

"It was *you*!" Connie screamed at Lanier. "It had to be you!"

"I swear! I didn't trash him!" Lanier cried. "Christ! Even this cop could see it couldn't be me! *He* was my only out from the jefe!"

Nick wondered if he'd taken that from what Ben had

said – or if there was more of this to come.

Chapter eight

"Let's get your full statement first, then we'll discuss where we go from there," Paddy said to Lanier. They were in Paddy's office after the mess at the Johns' house was finished. "This is Nick's case, so any deals are with him."

"I want the state attorney and DEA, not you," Lanier insisted stubbornly. "I ain't making any statement."

"Just take him back to a cell," Nick said disgustedly. "He can be transferred to the state lockup until his trial. Judge Collins will deny bail on this one. We've got plenty for a conviction.

"It's not their case. I've already told you DeGulio's covered all the way in this. The state attorney comes in automatically – *after* you're transferred."

"He can get me in the state pen! You got to give me protection! DEA will deal!"

"Protection from what?" Paddy asked innocently. "As Nick said, we have enough to convict you. You should be safe enough in the state penal institution where you'll be kept."

"That'll be Miami Regional, won't it?" Nick asked. Paddy saw the look in Nick's eye and bit off his retort about the closer facilities.

"Miami?" Lanier asked weakly. "But he's *there*!"

"Whatever are you talking about?" Paddy asked. "If you make a statement that would tend to indicate you need of any kind of protection it will be tendered. If you make no statement our hands are tied."

"I won't deal with anyone but either the state or DEA!"

Paddy slammed his hand over the tape recorder microphone and snarled, "Then you pays your dime and you takes your chances, don't you, you halfassed idiot punk!?"

He lifted his hand and said, in a very mild and reasonable tone, "Oh, sorry! Move it farther over that way, please. We don't want any gaps!"

Lanier sweated a minute longer, then Paddy called for the cell warden.

"Okay! I'll give a statement, but you got to guarantee protection from DeGulio! Otherwise, no deal!" Lanier said as the warden guard opened the door to look in for orders.

"Would you be so kind as to ask my secretary, Sgt. Blevins, to bring her pad?" Paddy asked. "If she would also bring coffee and cups for all of us, I would greatly appreciate it."

He nodded and went out. Lanier put his hand over the Mike and said, "You got to keep DeGulio away from me!"

"Pancho's in Boca Raton right now. I'll guarantee he'll leave you alone – *if* we get a true statement from you and if you don't do anything more to involve him."

Marsha came in with a tray of cups, sugar, cream, and spoons. There was a large pot of coffee on the tray with her notebook.

"You bunch of honky chauvinist pigs are going to hear from IA about your racial sexist demands for me to be your damned private waitress! I'll have you know I am a trained professional!"

"Professional what?" Paddy asked innocently.

"I left that one wide open, didn't I? What's the skinny? You got the recorder right there, so what's with the manual labor bit?"

"Mr. Lanier – or Carver – or whatever – wishes to tender a statement," Paddy answered. "Help yourself to the coffee, Mr. – Whatever."

Lanier glared and poured himself a cup. Marsha sat

across from him with her pen and notepad at the ready. Paddy heaved himself from his perch on the corner of the table and worked his bulk into a chair. Nick slowly stirred his coffee.

"Well?" Marsha finally said.

"Do you wish to simply make a general statement starting from whenever this mess began or do you want us to spend several hours questioning you?" Paddy asked pleasantly.

Lanier shrugged.

Nick suggested, "Just start from when you first heard about what you came here for. Include the DeGulio part."

"I never had any deal with DeGulio. I never even knew it was his stuff 'til I had it. It was too late, then.

"You know about the three families. (Paddy raised an eyebrow at Nick. Three? They knew about Doniletti and Farris.) Ben Johns used to be involved with all of them in one way or another. He was the drop-off for the wash.

"It was the Connie Terrell broad who roped him in for that. Her first husband was with one of the families. Doniletti.

"Anyhow, Johns found a way out. He never had the guts for the business anyway. He's a wimp.

"The people I worked for at the time set me up as a physical therapy instructor. I always worked out a lot and knew all about that kind of stuff, so it was easy.

"I came down here and went to where Johns and that bunch were moving into that big castle he bought. Terrell and Fields were in a sort of gym thing in Chi, so I laid a line about having worked there a little and saw they were moving down here and seeing as I was now living here they could maybe use an instructor.

"That was the first time I met that Emily broad and I

talked with her with them. She's really kinda special, you know? Smart, classy, and a knockout.

"Women can't resist me (Marsha almost laughed in his face), so they hired me to sort of be their instructor.

"The Shelly woman joined and so did Larson who I'd seen before up north. He didn't recognize me, so I could work it real good.

"I screwed up there because he *did* recognize me, but I didn't know that 'til a couple of days ago.

"I wondered why they brought the stuff to me and thought it was because the Terrell broad but she *didn't* recognize me because she'd never even seen me. Somebody else saw me, I figured, but then – anyhow, things went right along for a long time. Johns was really staying out of it and I had it real good. I was making some good geetus for laying around doing nothing much. I had the broads anytime I wanted. They'd sneak away for what you might call `Special instructions,' if you get me.

"Except Emily. She decided she had it too good with the wimp. That drove me crazy! I always want the wrong broad! It's always somebody who wants to get something out of me!

"She sort of let me know I could have her and everything else if I'd do a little side job for her, so I started making plans to get rid of the wimp."

"Wait a minute!" Nick interrupted. "Emily Johns made a deal for you to get rid of her husband?"

"She's too smart to do it directly. I'd, like, make little suggestions now and then and she'd let me know where the bread was buttered."

Nick didn't believe it! Emily was the only one in that bunch he liked, other than Lily. "Give us a couple examples."

"Well, I'd say something like, `You could use some work on your back.' Give a sign with your eyes like this (he got a droopy look and Marsha sniggered – which he seemed to take as some kind of excitement in her) and she'd say something maybe like, `With someone like Ben around, I'm going to take instructions from *you*?'

"You can see plain as day! Trash him and she's mine!

"See, she didn't want to take any chances he'd find out. She'd lose all the dough, and she's really smart, like I said, so she would never say anything direct, like. I had to work it so she could be guaranteed she'd keep the geetus and I'd have her!

"I'd say something subtle, like, `It's such a sunshiny day, why not go out on the boat and lay around?' and she'd come back with, `You're right! I think I'll go out on my *husband's* boat with my *husband*!'

"Plain as the nose on your face! Get rid of the wimp and I get both her *and* the boat.

"Things like that. Real plain. Not direct, but plain as a sore thumb!

"I saw his mother, Sara, had everything in her name there when they were talking one day and I was sorta hanging around by the door, so I knew I had to get rid of her first."

"I see," Nick said. "Go on."

"Yeah! Women always do that kind of thing. They can't leave me alone, but she's real smart. Don't take no chances. A couple months ago this Carlos guy comes and says seeing as how I used to work for some, uh, special people in Chi and Motown maybe I'd like to pick up some extra spending geetus. All I had to do was hold some stuff a couple of weeks 'til the big distributor was back from down south in Peru.

"Seeing as you know all about that end anyhow, it's

Alanza. For the record, you know.

"I was gonna make a deal with DEA about the way they handle it but they already know, so, you got to protect me anyhow, because I'm telling you this, so I'll give it to you for the record sorta so you can't say I held back anything that way.

"What they do, Alanza goes down and makes a deal DEA knows all about, but he never has anything on him and nobody can figure out how they're working it because that whole bunch are so dumb they hurt. They concentrate on watching him but the stuff comes in the day before he even goes south! The jefe has it here somewhere, then he comes back, and the DEA watches everything that comes in after! Really *dumb*! Even I could figure that after a couple times, I bet!

"When he gets back he has his organization to start putting the stuff out to distributors, so all they know he went, he came back, he's clean as a dog's tooth and all of a sudden this stuff is going out! It drives them nuts trying to figure how he works it when it was worked before he ever went south! Like, add it up and you can see what's going on, right? Even I can figure that, but the DEA runs around whining and crying that ... well. That Jessup character's a real half-brained doofus, anyhow. He makes up his mind Alanza's carrying the stuff and nobody can tell him nothing different.

"I think the jefe thought that one up. They act like they're turf fighting and all that. They didn't ever know that DEA had it figured.

"Anyhow, I got the stuff and could see it was way more than anybody but DeGulio and Alanza could even get their hands on, so I can tell you I had the shit scared out of me by that! You don't ever fool with those two. Not *ever*! Alanza's pretty bad, but the jefe's somebody *nobody* can get around! Even Doniletti's scared shitless by him, because all he's gotta do is say is somethin' like those guys have displeased him, would you believe? Exit big bad Doniletti.

"I put the stuff in the freezer because nobody would move that stuff for months, so nobody would ever know it was even in there.

"Then a bag got missing. I didn't know who had it, so I was really caught in a hard place.

"See, I didn't know Larson Crud had made me from the first, so I suppose he saw me going into the freezer and figured it out. I didn't know that 'til you found the stuff in the plant room. He sure let everybody know then! When you said you were talking to the jefe he knew his ass was in a crack and the crack was going to snap shut and cut it off for him!

"I was home free then. I'd already gotten rid of Sara, and I could explain the missing stuff – but you said that about the jefe and I knew he'd get me – and there's no way out!"

"You left out a few things, didn't you?" Nick said after about a minute's silence. "First, what happened with Sara?"

"Her? I went upstairs when I knew she'd be coming up there. She was a feisty old broad. I knew she'd come to see what I was doing if she saw me up there, so I stood by the stairs 'til she got out of her elevator with my back to her. She came along and I went in by the stairs when she was only a couple yards away.

"She did just what I figured. She came in, so I just chopped her and dumped her down the stairs. Then I went down to the plant ladder and waited 'til the coast was clear and got out!

"I went maybe two feet from the stuff! Damn!"

"Hold it!" Nick demanded. "What about the gloves?"

"The gloves? I never took them off 'til I was on my boat. That would've been dumb!

"I hung around out there forever. There were never any sirens or anything, so I finally figured they didn't find her, so I went back in and you were there.

"I didn't know you were a cop, then."

"You didn't see the ambulance or forensics van?"

"I didn't stay too close. I thought there'd be sirens. That was some smack when I saw the chalk and didn't ever hear any sirens!"

"What about the gloves in the freezer?"

"I don't even know what the hell you're talking about! What the hell did...? What gloves in the freezer? Hell! I wasn't anywhere near the damned freezer then!"

"You didn't leave any gloves in the freezer when you went down to be sure Sara was dead?"

"Why the hell would I check? I *knew* she was *damned* dead! Hell! I'm an *expert*!"

Paddy looked at Nick, then at Marsha, then back to Nick.

"What did I miss?" Lanier asked, staring around at them.

"A loose end. You went up there to kill Sara and out? She didn't accidentally find you up there?"

"I just *said* I went up there so she'd find me!"

"What about the rest of it?" Nick asked tiredly. Now he had an unanswered question. That would keep him awake at night. "What rest of it? That's about all of it."

"Not quite!" Paddy interrupted. "You sort of seemed to leave out Larson!"

"I told you! I didn't know he made me. He took the stuff. I got in a crack about that.

"You found the stuff. So my ass got back in a crack

because the jefe doesn't like me and he'll use because I lost a bag to get even."

"Why did you kill him, then?"

"Jesus Christ! You said yourself he was my way out with DeGulio! I may screw up a lot, but I'm not *that* stupid! If he's dead, I got no out! I got no ... Oh for...! You meant you had me for that! I thought you meant about Sara! I sat here and spilled my guts, and it wasn't even for the right thing?

"Christ almighty! You said *yourself* how no jury would hang me for knocking over some cheap punk hood! I know where all his old skeletons are hid!

"Oh, cripes! I did it again!"

"Not really. I promised I'd protect you from Pancho. You have that now."

"How you figure to do that? And how come some cop calls Mr. DeGulio by his nickname? Not even Artie Doniletti would dare to do that!"

Nick picked up the phone and told the operator to give him a secure outside line. He hid the phone as he punched the number, waited, asked to speak to Pancho, gave his name, and waited another half minute.

"Nickie? What's the scam?" DeGulio answered.

"Hi, Pancho. I have Lanier. We'll put him away for a very long time, so do me a favor? Let us handle him? All the way?"

"If you'll keep me out of it. Done!"

"I have something else. Call it a favor for a favor."

"If he ratted anyone the deal's off – assuming the idiot actually knew anything – which I find more than unlikely. What?"

"He didn't do anything except add another piece to what was already there."

"Okay. What's the favor? Deal sticks."

"Don't use the Alanza connection again. Don't use the pattern again," Nick answered, as Paddy stared in shocked open-mouthed disbelief. "Some Jesse James figured it and will be there waiting next time."

"Done. I wondered when he'd catch it. It was getting a bit warm lately, so I'll stay out of it for awhile. Both sides can use a rest. Maybe the screwups will stop if we all get some rest, si?"

"Could be. Larson bought it."

"I know."

"It wasn't Lanier."

"I know."

Chapter nine

"So! You looked like you'd been smacked in the puss with a wet fish a couple of times in there," Marsha said as she finished typing the statement for Lanier to sign. "I could understand the one where he claimed he didn't kill that Larson character, but what's the big deal about those gloves?"

"It's really no problem," Nick assured her. "I'm sure it'll all be explained when I get Tiny's report about the dope we found in the atrium. I have to be sure about Larson now. That leaves me another murderer to find."

"Well, Paddy's not speaking to you. When you told DeGulio about knowing about Alanza I thought he'd die of apoplexy on the spot!"

"When he stops to think about it for a bit he'll come around. He knows damned well I wouldn't give anything away. Not something like that!"

Nick picked up the interphone to ask Frog to bring the tape he made at the atrium and to bring Tiny's report on the dope bag at the same time.

Paddy came out of his office and marched over to Nick. "He already knew it? That's why?"

"Pretty obviously. To Pancho, I was proving my word. He played along to let me off the hook about owing favors."

He picked up the phone and punched Jessup's number.

"You didn't check before?" Paddy asked.

Nick shook his head. "I didn't have to. If some twobit hood nobody trusted, like a certain Lanier, knew it, it was general knowledge," then into the phone, "Jess! Why didn't you tell me you knew about Alanza and DeGulio?"

Paddy shook his head.

"We didn't until we got that stuff from you. Chico

made that one phone call, then gave our man the slip. Alanza wasn't coming in until about an hour after you arrived, so Chico headed for DeGulio. He was an Alanza man, mostly. When you found him there where I sent you to get you out of my hair and just to see if you had the guts, it gave the show away.

"We were suspicious, but didn't have anything.

"How did they work it? You've gotten very cozy with the jefe, it seems. Be careful!"

"I will. I like Pancho. The stuff was in the day before Alanza went south to draw our attention away from DeGulio, who sent the stuff to a holder. They then waited for Alanza to come back for you to concentrate on to distribute the stuff.

"It's mostly a game of wits. It amused Pancho for you to be so exasperated and frustrated. Alanza was always clean, but the stuff started showing up right after he returned from a trip."

"It's no game to me!"

"It's no game to me, either. Not so much about the drugs themselves, but for what they do to people and what people do to get them. I see some results of that. Larson was trashed because he got involved with those people without knowing who they were.

"On the other hand, he was a cheap, violent hood. It couldn't have happened to a more deserving person."

"And the old woman? Did she deserve it?"

"That was a straight murder of a different sort. Believe it or not, that had nothing whatever to do with drugs. I don't think Larson's murder did either. I'll fax you a transcript of Lanier's statement."

"But ... why would Lanier kill Larson if it wasn't for the missing drugs?"

"He didn't kill Larson, according to him. I think I

believe him. I'll know definitely in a few more minutes."

They chatted a few minutes, then Nick hung up. Paddy read the statement and handed it to Nick, who read most of it before Frog wandered in. He nodded and gave it back to Marsha, who faxed a copy to Jessup, then took the original out to have Lanier sign it.

"What did I get that you have to see?" Frog asked, handing Nick Tiny's report on the dope.

As he was beginning to expect, the bag was clean of prints on the outside.

"Let's look at this videotape of you finding the drugs behind that trellis in Paddy's office. He has the big screen."

They went in and handed Paddy the videotape.

"Well? Did the analysis Tiny made come out as you expected?" Paddy asked.

"I think so. What I needed there was prints on the bag. There weren't any, so the gloves are explained if not much else is."

"They are? Oh," Paddy said.

"Right. Larson used them. He could as easily have taken them from the freezer as Lanier or anyone else. He used them again to hide the stuff in the trellis."

Frog started the videotape and they watched his view as he slowly approached the foot of the trellis, scanned around the area, and started up. He'd just found the bag and was holding the vines aside for a good shot when he suddenly dropped the vines and the view swept to the rail three feet above. The view went quickly up, over the rail, and along the hall.

"Freeze it there a second," Nick said, noting the empty hall. "I assume you looked up when she screamed. It took you about four seconds to make the rail and look down that hall.

"Go ahead now."

The door to Shelly's room flew open and Bart stepped out to look down the hall. He then ran toward Connie's room as the hall door to the bath opened and Nick burst from the stairway with his pistol ahead.

"Good enough," Nick said. "Back it up to where you first came over the rail."

Frog ran the tape back, then started it forward again.

Nick suddenly said, "Freeze!" as the first glance down the hall came on. The whole empty hall was visible.

"Okay. Connie went into the bath. This is about twenty seconds later. Allowing for ten seconds to kill Larson, there was about ... I think four or five seconds, leaving no more than four seconds to get to the rear stairway.

"Not even maybe. Lanier didn't have time to get to the stairs and close the door. He's right, so he didn't kill Larson."

"It could only be one other person," Frog said. "Her."

"No. There was enough time to get back to Shelly's room or to the bath. There was some blood on the killer, so it could have been Connie or Shelly. There was no trace of blood on Bart, so he's not the killer."

"There would be some blood on Shelly, though!" Paddy pointed out. "It had to be Connie."

"Shelly was using a hair dryer after washing her hair. She had that plastic thing on. It would keep the blood off of her."

"She didn't have it on when she came out of the door," Frog said, running the tape on.

"Exactly. She then took Connie to her bath to clean her up, so they got blood on a lot of things. It was one or both of them."

"How do you find out which one?" Paddy asked.

"I think that won't be too difficult. It's a matter of

motive again.

"Who had one?"

"Neither of them!" Paddy cried. "What are you trying to pull now? Connie was his lover, but there's no evidence of problems. You've established that Shelly didn't have any connection to him, and.... I see."

"See what?" Marsha asked, coming in the door.

"Why Connie killed Larson," Frog answered.

"Why?" Marsha asked, looking at Nick.

"We were looking for a motive. Nobody had one except maybe Lanier, and he didn't do it – but Connie could be ordered to get rid of him. All we have to do now is prove the Doniletti group still has her under control."

"Why?" Paddy demanded.

"The very same reason that Lanier's scared shitless of DeGulio!" Marsha answered. "He grabbed that dope that turned out to be DeGulio's property!"

"Even worse," Nick added. "It was a sack of dope that belonged to DeGulio, but that Doniletti was responsible for. The fact Larson grabbed it could start a war among the families – particularly seeing they'll feel that gave their scam with Alanza away. All three families could end up in a wild vendetta. Alanza against Farris against Doniletti, and all combinations of same – which means DeGulio was never more than ... this is weird. Now I don't know what's going on again. How could Pancho hold that power?

"I'm on a tangent.

"To show good faith Farris had to sacrifice Larson to Doniletti. That would show that they weren't behind it. It's just the way they do business. They all thought – Connie included – it would be easy to hang it on Lanier, then they'd drop back and regroup."

"How're you gonna prove it?" Frog asked. "You're the one who doesn't make sense again."

"They didn't give her the order to kill him through mental damned telepathy! They had no reason to believe we'd ever check little things like phone calls. We'd think it was tied up tight to Lanier. If Frog hadn't looked over that rail so quickly it would have worked, at least to the extent we could never be sure."

Marsha grabbed the phone and called the phone company, then they waited twenty five minutes for the fax to come in. There were seven calls from out of the local area. Only the numbers.

Nick dialed the first one. It was a northern real estate brokerage office returning a call from Ben Johns. He was trying to sell the old family place in Detroit. It was the real estate agency he owned.

The second was a pawn shop reporting last month's receipts.

The third was from Bart Fields' sister in Brookhaven, Conn.

The fourth was the other pawn shop reporting.

The fifth was from Clarke, Smith, Bills, and Co. Inc., stockbrokers, NYC.

The sixth was the first pawn shop again, so Nick didn't call them back.

The seventh was from a Mrs. Robert Johnson calling to offer her condolences to Ben and Emily on the loss of Ben's mother.

"What now?" Paddy asked.

"I can pull a bluff or we can see who's behind that brokerage firm. It'll be that one."

"Let me try something," Marsha said. She picked up the phone and dialed the NY number.

"I'm calling with a message from Constance Terrell?"

she said after a minute. "I'm to speak with Smith?"

She winked and waited, then said, "Listen! Connie said to call this number and to tell Smith he was not to answer any questions about your call yesterday! She can't leave the house and can't use the phone there. She said you really screwed up calling her because they *did* check and they're asking all the wrong questions about all the wrong things!"

"She has a perfectly legitimate account here, so tell her we can say we called to tell her to dump her J. R. Reynolds and purchase Apple/ MacIntosh.

"Have you got that? We'll retro a buy-purchase for that. She dumped Reynolds and bought MacIntosh."

"Hey! I'm just the maid! I don't know from no stocks! I only called you because she couldn't get anybody else to call and she gave me a hundred bucks to call and clam about it!"

"Tell her we'll handle it!" Smith demanded.

Marsha slammed the phone down and grinned. "It was them! I knew it would have to be somebody named Smith. They aren't the most original thinkers on the planet."

Nick called the NYCPD infonet and asked about the firm. They'd get back in half an hour, so it was time to wait again.

"We *do* have all these great electronic gimmicks to do most of the legwork part for us," Paddy said. "We're almost unnecessary anymore!"

They chatted until the call came. Clarke, Smith, and Bills, and Co. was mostly a loan sharking operation used against small businesses, but they did stay barely within the law by trading a few stocks. Vincente and Paulo Doniletti were charter members of the board of trustees. The only really new thing they learned was that it was those two, not the Arturo Doniletti group, who she had been involved with. Arturo, the big Doniletti, seemed to stay away from any major involvement with drugs – a minor point in his favor, considering other parts of his business.

"That will do it!" Nick said. "Let's go pick her up!" He went out to his car. Frog said he'd ride along.


"Mrs. Constance Terrell, I am here to place you under arrest for the murder of David Larson in the first degree. Anything you say can and will be used against you in a court of law. You have the right to have an attorney present for the tendering of any testimony. If you cannot afford an attorney the court will appoint one to act on your behalf. Do you understand these rights?"

"ARE YOU MAD!?" she yelled. "LANIER killed David!"

"No way. His alibi is unbreakable. I must warn you not to speak. We have solid evidence."

"What kind of evidence?" Emily, who accompanied them up to Connie's new room, asked.

"You saw Frog on the atrium trellis near the top when Mrs. Terrell screamed?" Nick asked. She nodded.

"He had the video camera on his head. He looked down that hall as he looked over the railing. There was no one there until Mr. Fields ran out from Miss Johns' room, then Miss Johns and I entered eight seconds later. Mr. Lanier came from the rear stairs five seconds after that. It's all on the tape."

"I don't see...?"

"There simply was not time for Mr. Lanier to have left that room and made it to the rear stairs before Mr. Forest taped the view down the hall. An Olympic sprinter probably couldn't have done it. We have a police videotape that proves *no one* left that room in the necessary time frame. Only Mrs. Terrell and Mr. Larson were in that room. It isn't possible for a person to inflict that kind of wound on himself, so Mrs. Terrell is the only *possible* perpetrator."

"I could be wrong about how long it took me to go in there and come back out!" Connie cried.

"Mrs. Terrell! Please! For your own good, be quiet! You were given your rights in front of witnesses!"

"We also have the call from Smith in New York. You were ordered to get rid of Larson. You never stopped working for the Doniletti family. You didn't have the way Mr. Johns did to enforce any such thing. The ownership of such companies is in public records.

"Vincente and Paulo Doniletti are charter members and officers of that company. You may wish to implicate them or not. My job is solely to discover and arrest a murderer here in this county.

"Mr. Forest will accompany you to collect a few things.

"Frog, she coldbloodedly slashed her own lover's throat in a room right down the hall. Don't forget that for one split second if you want to make your date with Ann Saturday night!"

"I wondered," Emily said. "I could see there wasn't time. As soon as I knew there were drugs involved I remembered Connie's first husband. There really wasn't time, Connie."

"Let's go," Nick said.

C. D. Moulton's works are available on most major outlets as printed or e-books. CD writes the CD Grimes, PI, mysteries, the Det. Lt. Nick Storie mysteries, the Clint Faraday mysteries, the Flight of the Maita science fiction series, books on orchid culture and many others of many types. Mystery, adventure, intrigue, science fiction, humor, fantasy, paranormal, mild erotica, and factual.

C. D. Moulton's works are available on most major outlets as printed or e-books. CD writes the CD Grimes, PI, mysteries, the Det. Lt. Nick Storie mysteries, the Clint Faraday mysteries, the Flight of the Maita science fiction series, books on orchid culture and many others of many types. Mystery, adventure, intrigue, science fiction, humor, fantasy, paranormal, mild erotica, and factual.